Dead End Street

R.L. Herron

Other Books by R.L. Herron

REICHOLD STREET
2012 Readers' Favorite Gold Medal Winner
Book I of the Series

……...

ZEBULON and Other Short Stories
2013 Readers' Favorite Silver Medal Winner

……...

TINKER and Other Short Stories

……...

ONE WAY STREET
Book II of the Reichold Street Series
2014 Readers' Favorite 5-Stars

……...

STREET LIGHT
Book III of the Reichold Street Series
2015 Readers' Favorite 5-Stars
2015 Shelf Unbound Notable 100 Book

BLOOD LAKE
2016 Readers' Favorite Bronze Medal Winner
2016 Shelf Unbound Notable 100 Book

DEDICATION

There's no individual specifically cataloged as one of the many fictional characters populating my work, although bits and pieces of several may have come from real people I've known, met or seen. It's something I think most fiction authors will do.

One of my personal favorite characters in this series, *Puz*, was assembled, in part, from vague recollections of a childhood friend I lost track of decades ago. I put together a few mannerisms for the character from thoughts of him stuck somewhere in the dark recesses of my mind.

I wasn't consciously thinking about him while I wrote the stories, and I didn't use any actual life events, but he's there nonetheless. Now, whenever I conjure *Puz* in my mind's eye, I see my friend. I can't help it.

However, because of our decades long disconnect, he's forever in my memory as he was at seventeen...the last time I saw him.

When I finished the third novel, I decided the time had come to look him up. I thought it would be interesting to talk to him again and perhaps give him a copy of the books a few of his idiosyncrasies had managed to sneak into. I was looking forward to it, because I knew the *Puz* character would give him a really good laugh.

After all this time, thanks to the Internet, the search for my old friend was far easier than I thought it would be. It was actually quite successful. Believe it or not, I found him on the very first day.

Alas, like many things that happen to those of us who procrastinate, I was much too late to talk to him again. The listing I found for him was an obituary.

My old friend Kenneth Edward Riddle passed away in June 2009. I can't tell you how awful that discovery felt. It wasn't just the shock of his passing. It was the realization of all the years I let go by without keeping in touch.

There were memories of a lifetime I wanted to share, but no longer could. It was as simple, and as difficult, as that. I really wanted to talk to him again. To listen to his infectious laugh. To see him smile. To hear him say, one more time, *"Wassup?"*

Since that is now impossible, this book is dedicated to his memory, with my sincere, if terribly belated, thanks for his friendship.

"The violets in the mountains have broken the rocks."

~ Tennessee Williams

PROLOGUE

My first novel, *Reichold Street*, about a group of friends growing up during the turbulent 1960s Vietnam era, is set in a fictional working-class town. It was fun to write and it evolved into a series...but, contrary to what my Gentle Readers may think, it wasn't something I planned. It just happened.

Once the characters were set in motion, they often had their own stories to tell, and they quite often startled and amazed even yours truly with the things they did.

In the prologue to *"Street Light,"* the third book in the series, I said writing fiction is often a whole bunch of happy surprises like that. When that book was finished, I went on to writing other things, because it seemed like the tale was over...although I remember telling my bride it remained to be seen if the gang from Brickdale had more to tell us.

It looks like they did.

An excerpt from ...

REICHOLD STREET
2012 Readers' Favorite Gold Medal Winner

It was late August, 1962, when I first saw Albert Parker. After all this time, I still remember the year quite distinctly. It was my second teenage summer and, like discovering I had a sexual identity, it was a part of life's first great transition. I had been waiting for months for something special to happen, something magical. Something like having Marilyn Monroe show up on my doorstep.

In my dreams, she would be wearing that flouncy white dress she wore over the subway grate in *The Seven Year Itch*. She would lean close and ask me, in one of her breathless whispers, to *take her*. At the time, I wasn't even sure what that meant.

Hell, it didn't matter. Just having her show up would have been enough, as long as the gang saw her. Of course, Marilyn never came to 752 Reichold Street in Brickdale.

Albert did....

An excerpt from …

ONE WAY STREET
2014 Readers' Favorite 5-Star Review

"What was his name?" Blake turned to look at me. He had blacked his face for camouflage and muddy streaks were caked on top of it. He could have been a clown, if he smiled. Or the devil himself, if he was angry.

"Albert Parker," I said, "He used to live right across the street from me."

"Good guy?"

I thought about it a moment. "Yeah," I said, looking over at Blake, "a really good guy."

"You said he used to live across the street. Did he move, or something?"

"No," I said, "he died."

"Aw, that's too bad, man," Blake said. He adjusted his bandolier and started to lean back against the mound of dirt behind us. "What'd he die from?"

"Coming over here."

An excerpt from ...

STREET LIGHT
2015 Readers' Favorite 5-Star Review and
Shelf Unbound's 100 Notable Books of 2015

"You know I'm always a hundred percent square with you, Micah...always." His voice had a high girlie squeak to it. A squeak I liked. The squeak of fear.

"Still," I said, so low it was almost a hiss, "It's a tempting load of twenties, isn't it?"

"Ain't enough to get gutted over," Philly said.

His eyes never left the knife in my hand.

I smiled at Philly again.

"Right as rain, cousin..." I said, grinning, "...right as rain." I flicked the super sharp blade and nicked the ball of Philly's thumb. A small trickle of blood ran down his arm and dripped on the linoleum.

"Ouch," Philly said as he jerked away.

"See that it always stays that way," I said, giving him the evil red eye as I peeled another twenty out of the stack on the table in front of me.

"Damn it, Micah," Philly said, holding the new cut on his hand. He looked up at me right after he said it. His eyes were as wide and frightened as those of a fat boar who's just seen the leopard's teeth beneath his throat.

And now...

Dead End Street

CHAPTER 1 – Paul Barrett

They say a dead end street is a good place to turn around, because there's not much else you can do there. The first time I heard that phrase it made a lot of sense to me. Now, I'm not so sure.

There was already so much in my life I needed to forget, when I was invited to return to Brickdale for Randy and Janice's wedding, just looking at their invitation made my hands shake. I wasn't sure being in my old hometown again was going to help anything at all. The thought of going back to face my friends and all the memories they, and that town, invoked, felt a bit like planning to head down one of those dead-end streets...going the wrong way.

Don't get me wrong. I was far from certain my new location in California was any better. To me, both places had turned into dead ends, but there was no turnaround space at either one. I complained about it often to my poor agent, and anyone else who would listen.

I'd only been back to Brickdale a few times since my father moved us away in the late 60s. One was to try to talk my friend, Albert Parker, out of his decision to join the Marines. Randy Camron had called and pleaded with me to make that effort. "You gotta do something, Paulie," he said, "Albert's shipping out soon."

"I don't think it'll do any good," I said.

"You're the only chance the SOB's got now."

"I'm his only chance?" I couldn't believe he'd said that. "Since when did Albert's fate become my problem?"

"You know you're the only one he ever had any respect for," Randy said. "I've already tried to tell him he's being an asshole, but do you really think he listens to me?"

"What makes you think he'll listen any better to me?"

Randy's sigh was like a small tornado. "You're probably right," he said, "but you can't let him do this without trying to stop him. Even Albert deserves something better."

He was right about that, so I tried...but Albert was as bull-headed as I thought he might be. It's why I had to go back in less than two years to attend his funeral.

The world being the way it was, soon after Albert was killed, I got myself immersed in the same horrific conflict in Vietnam. I came home pretty well traumatized. Like a lot of the guys who made it back, I don't talk about it much. The few times I've ever mentioned it, people were very quick to point out I had volunteered. I guess in their minds that made the trauma something of my own doing. They may be right...I don't really know. I probably care even less.

It doesn't change any of my feelings about it. All things considered, I felt fortunate to have survived the depression that stalked me when I came home.

Finding Carrie had been a big part of my salvation.

My war buddy, Blake Thompson, wasn't so lucky. I still recall the night we shared a foxhole in that God-forsaken piece of the planet near the *A Shau Valley* when he showed me his girlfriend's picture. From the dreamy look on his face I could tell he idolized his Brenda, but she not only spurned him when he came home...she spat on him.

In a long, rambling letter, Blake told me how he'd shot her and the new boy he'd found her with. I honestly don't think he could help his reaction. Disbelief and rage got the best of him, and his mental anguish over that horrific deed must have unleashed something really terrible in his soul. I thought, at the time, his letter was a suicide note. In a way, I suppose it was. I think he knew very well where his actions would lead.

Blake, for some reason, had added me to his list of people he thought were responsible for the disrespect he felt, or had been witnesses to his madness. So, it was because of me Carrie came into harm's way.

My sweet Carrie never knew the facts behind the auto accident that ended her life. I've often wished I'd never recognized the whole truth myself. When I discovered my old army buddy was responsible, it almost crushed my will to go on. I didn't think my heart could hold so much grief and hate at the same time and still survive. I made what I thought was my last trip to Brickdale shortly after Carrie's death, looking for solace I couldn't find.

When the FBI finally shot Blake in my house in Rancho Santa Fe, an odd thing happened. Even though he had come there to kill me, when I saw Blake lying dead on the floor, with a look on his face that seemed both surprised and afraid, the memory of an old Brickdale neighbor popped into my head.

CHAPTER 2

Actually, it was the memory of Everett Doughton's vicious little bastard of a dog that resurrected itself. Everett lived about three houses down from us on Reichold Street, and he had a nasty beast he kept chained up in his back yard.

I remember him telling my father he bought the dog for security, but I think it was really just to keep kids from chasing baseballs into his yard. He hated to have kids trampling all over his meticulously manicured grass and the flowerbeds where he grew his roses, so he bought the most ill-tempered beast he could find. He kept it on a long, bright chain anchored to the middle of his back yard.

I don't remember what he actually called it, but every kid in the neighborhood had a special name for it.

We called it *T-Rex.*

That black Rottweiler, with its mahogany maw full of sharp, snarling teeth, was to become one of the main terrors of our lives. Particularly on days when it got loose.

I hated that mutt.

However, it wasn't the only neighborhood terror. As funny as it seems, another one was Old Lady Morris, the spinster who lived at the end of the block.

If she had a first name, I never knew it. To me, and the rest of the kids on the block she was always *Old Lady Morris*. Her shrill voice, which could seem about three octaves higher than a fire alarm, screamed incessantly when we played anywhere near her house.

I was certain she simply hated to see kids having fun. However, it was for another reason entirely that she and *T-Rex* are both intimately entwined in my memory.

She was so withered and tiny she could scarcely see over the steering wheel of her '58 Buick Roadmaster, but you could count on her driving that old behemoth down the street with the accelerator pedal pressed to the floor.

She did it so often all the guys were sure she actually got her kicks breaking up our street baseball games...and watching us all dive for the curb to get out of her way.

The day she hit T-Rex, even though I would have sworn she was laughing as she sped past, I'd be lying if I said it wasn't frightening. The horrendous sound of screeching brakes, followed by a dull thump and the screams of kids, are seared forever in my memory.

At first, I thought she'd run over one of my friends. When I realized it was only T-Rex, who had somehow gotten loose and raced into the street just in time to meet his fate, my mood became almost joyous.

No more lost baseballs over Doughten's lousy fence!

However, when I saw the beast up close, lying broken and bloody in the middle of the street, my old hatred totally dissolved. The poor thing on the pavement didn't look like the snarling demon we had all feared. It was just a poor mangled, dying dog.

Looking at Blake after the FBI shot him had been like that. I understood, all too well, how he could have imagined the world had been conspiring against him. My hatred for what he had done was replaced by a profound concern for what he'd been through.

It was trying to reconcile that deep empathy with the emptiness I'd felt ever since Carrie's accident that led to the most miserable depression I've ever known. It had taken a long time to get over all the miserable things that had happened since the war, and as much as I enjoyed my friends, I honestly wasn't sure I could face it all again.

It was my literary agent, Roger Craig, who talked me into going to the wedding. Like my Brickdale friends, fate also had him there during the confrontation with Blake in Rancho Santa Fe. He also knew about all the demons I'd been fighting before that, and thought it would be good for me to get away from all the bad memories for a while.

God knows there are a lot of them.

"C'mon, Paul," he pleaded, "it'll be good for you."

Roger turned the whole thing into a book-signing tour, so the publisher would pay for the trip, thinking that would force me to go. He even volunteered to ride with me on the corporate plane, because I was worried about going alone.

My nerves were on edge and I didn't say much to him on the trip across country but, when we actually got to Brickdale, I started to think maybe his decision might have been a good one, after all.

It was really nice to see my old friends again, now that the war and all the crazy nonsense with Blake seemed so far behind. I thought I'd had more than enough of the place, but it seemed Roger had been right to get me to go back.

"Thanks for talking me into coming," I told him, trying not to sound patronizing, "You were right, as usual."

He just smiled.

Unfortunately, the good feelings didn't last very long.

It wasn't Randy and Janice's fault. What should have been a beautiful, relaxing evening with them became instead the wedding reception from Hell.

A local druggie, who harbored some sort of grudge against Randy and his brother, became yet another cast member in the odd menagerie of phantasms that, over the years, had seemed to march at will through my dreams.

The whole thing was such a traumatic experience I once again felt vastly relieved just to have survived. When the

Sheriff's witness interrogation was over, I packed up as fast as I could and left.

It was a bizarre time, but being with all my friends through the worst of it and coming out whole, I realized a surprising thing...I finally also felt some small degree of closure about what had happened to Carrie.

I even poured my heart out to Janice about it before I went home. Unfortunately, I failed miserably at forgetting.

There are some who just don't understand how very difficult that can be. There are some things that just can't be easily forgotten and, take it from me, those persistent memories do not feel good at all. Not one little bit.

For weeks after their reception, I thought about calling Janice when my memories threatened to overwhelm me. I knew she would understand...probably far better than most...she'd already been through so much.

However, I decided not to bother her with my problems. She'd seen enough shit in her life without burdening her with mine. We all know shit happens. It's an integral part of life that we all have to learn to deal with.

Besides, I was also sure Randy wouldn't want me calling his wife all the time anyway.

CHAPTER 3

R oger insisted on occupying the seat directly across the aisle coming home from the wedding, despite the fact we were still the only two passengers on the plane and there was plenty of room.

"It'll give us a chance to talk," he said, as he plunked down in the seat. With little more introduction than that, he began to recant virtually everything that had just happened to us. Almost all of it had already joined the ranks of things I'd just as soon forget.

In fact, before we ever set foot in the plane, I had repeatedly told him I wasn't going to discuss events from that miserable wedding reception. So, I was a little ticked when he did that, and it showed when I interrupted him.

"Talk about what, Roger?"

"The wedding from Hell," he said, "What else?"

"You don't listen very well, do you?" There was venom in my voice. I was more than a little put out with him.

"It won't go away by ignoring it," Roger said, and despite my repeated admonitions otherwise, we spent an inordinate amount of time recounting all the horrifying incidents of that awful day. Roger did most of the talking.

At times, he sounded like a broken record, repeating his inane observations over and over. I couldn't shut him up. I suppose it was his way of coping.

"I wish things had worked out better for Randy and Janice," I finally said, trying hard to hold up my end of the conversation. "Neither one of them deserved to have their wedding day turn out like that." A long sigh escaped me. "They're good people, and they've already been through their share of Hell."

Roger agreed with a nod. "I'm glad they're okay."

"Me too."

A long silence followed.

Roger spoke again first, and when he did his eyes had a far away, restless, almost haunted look...and his voice was barely above a whisper.

"That Micah had to be the scariest man I've ever seen."

I didn't know what to say. My own head throbbed when I thought about the awful events we had recently survived. Wiping perspiration from my upper lip, I finally managed to mumble a few words between my fingers.

"Is that counting the *Shadow Man?*"

Roger took a deep, abrupt breath that almost sounded like a gasp. "Blake Thompson certainly comes in a close second, no doubt about that," he said with a long, drawn out exhalation, "but yes...even counting him."

As soon as he said that, I remembered Roger had lived through those horrific times with *both* Blake and Micah. He hadn't been in Vietnam with me, but with just those two he'd certainly seen enough horror to add to his own share of nightmares.

I was thoroughly ashamed for thinking only of myself, but couldn't imagine the right words to say to him to make it any better. Instead, I sat back in my seat, listened to the drone of the plane's engines and looked at Roger's disheveled tangle of salt-and-pepper hair. As I tried to collect my jumbled thoughts, I realized I was grateful for his friendship and wondered how I could have been so self-centered.

"I've put you through a lot since you met me," I finally said. "I wouldn't blame you a bit for walking away."

Another awkward silence followed my words to him. Instead of answering right away, Roger took a slow, deep breath, sat back in his own seat and seemed to study me for several long moments.

"There have been some extremely good times since we met, too," he finally said. "Don't forget that."

"Yeah, sure," I said, almost barking my response. I was being dismissive and I knew it, because I still felt awkward and didn't really want to talk.

Roger gave me a barely audible grunt...but that quick sound, and the shadowy, dark look in his eyes, conveyed his annoyance quite well.

"Okay," I said, feeling guilty again, "like what?"

Roger took another deep breath and seemed to sit up a little taller in his seat.

"Like selling your first book," he answered, without any hesitation, "that was a high point in my life, too."

"Yeah..." I said, still in a condescending tone, "...right."

I started to say more, but before I could speak, Roger took another deep breath and continued.

"Getting you that fabulous advance was nice. I made a bundle, too, don't forget." I tried to interrupt him without success. He held up his hand to stop me. "Having your books hit the best-seller list," he said, smiling a little, "How cool was that? Don't you think I felt justified for my faith in you then? Getting you that absolutely incredible advance for more, *ahem*, as yet unwritten sequels..."

Roger had ticked off those individual items on the fingers of his left hand, pausing after he mentioned each one. He was looking right at me when he added Carrie's name, hesitantly, as if he was almost reluctant to say it.

"Roger..." I whispered. I sat forward in my seat, trying to get him to stop. "Please don't."

My eyes had gotten misty when he mentioned Carrie and it was so hard for me to speak that, when I did, my voice was so quiet I wasn't at all sure he could hear me.

"What?" he said, I thought confirming my suspicion, "Did I leave anything out?"

My breathing was slow and shallow when I answered him. I leaned across the aisle and touched his arm.

"I miss her," I said. "She was the best thing that ever happened to me."

I could tell Roger felt awkward, not so much by what he said, but by the way he suddenly stood up in the aisle. He glanced at the door to the pilot's cabin, self-consciously jingling the keys in his pocket. He paced a few steps forward, then returned with his eyes downcast and immediately tried to change the subject.

"Have you got that re-write finished?" he said, trying to sound as if the status of my writing career had been what we were talking about all along.

"You know I don't."

"The publisher doesn't care about all the shit we just went through, you know," he said, looking back again at the door to the pilot's cabin, as if hoping it would open and relieve him of the task of talking. "They're going to be all over you when we get back. Literally all over you...I can promise you that."

I couldn't speak, but then I didn't have to. When he saw the tears running down my cheeks, Roger knew he'd hit the sore spot in my heart, without me having to say a word. "I know, my friend," he added, his voice as soft as I'd ever heard him say anything, "I know. I miss her, too."

I still couldn't answer him, and I certainly didn't want him waxing sentimental for the rest of the trip, so I closed my eyes. He called my name a few times, but I pretended to be dozing. I'm sure Roger knew it was a ruse on my part, but he sat down again and left me alone.

In the silence, I could hear his own quiet weeping, and knew he was probably as grateful as I was there was no one else on the plane.

CHAPTER 4

T hat self-enforced silence continued until we began the descent into San Diego International. I felt the change in airspeed and opened my eyes just as Roger tapped me on the shoulder.

"Better buckle up," he said. "Lindbergh Field is dead ahead. The pilot just announced he's getting ready to make the approach. We'll be landing in a few minutes."

I fumbled with my seat belt and silently watched the airfield grow larger as we descended. I could see the Bay off to our left and, still thinking about Carrie, I had a sudden, scary mental desire for the plane to crash, so I could join her. It was the first time the thought happened to me, although my grief was as strong as it ever had been. It passed almost as fast as it came, but my hands were trembling when I looked at Roger.

If he noticed my trembling, he didn't say anything. I jumped a little when we touched down, even though the landing was without the slightest jar. He nodded at me and I tried to smile, but resisted the urge to comment.

As we taxied to the private hanger where the plane was stored, I couldn't look directly at him. I was afraid of my feelings and didn't want him to see tears again. I was already up and walking down the aisle when the pilot came out of the cockpit to open the fuselage door. I shook hands and thanked him for an uneventful flight.

Roger was right behind me.

I could hear him doing exactly the same thing as I went down the ladder and ducked under the wing to pick up my things. Roger eventually caught up to me and we stood together, silent.

Not speaking a word as we waited for the handlers to unload our luggage wasn't a particularly graceful moment, but our lack of conversation was fine with me. I didn't think the awkwardness would last very long, and didn't really care if it did. I was doing my best to ignore everyone.

Roger's bags were unloaded first. I watched him pick them up and start toward the parking area. I was a few paces behind him. Our cars were side-by-side in the parking lot on the far side of the hanger, so we were headed in the same direction, but from there we were going our separate ways. I was already thinking about the drive home when I saw Roger hesitate and look back at me.

"Are you all right to go home alone?" he said. He put his bags down as he waited for my answer.

Catching up to him, I rolled my eyes at his comment and used the nickname I'd given to him. "What do you think, *Dodger*," I said, "Do I look like I'm three? Or do I just suddenly strike you as totally incompetent?"

I wiped my cheek, in case there was still a tear.

"That was uncalled for, my friend."

I had a sharp response ready for him, one I knew had some bite to it, but when I looked up and saw the serious concern on his face, I couldn't make myself say it. With my lips pursed tight, I turned away and started walking again.

Without a word, he did, too.

More or less side-by-side, we remained silent as we walked across the apron in front of the open hanger door. We went together around the building to our cars, and I could feel him watching me.

I reached mine first. Knowing he was still watching and waiting, I put my suitcase away and closed the deck lid. Sighing, still without a word, I turned to face him.

"You're right," I mumbled, "that was totally uncalled for. You're a good friend, Roger. Forget I got so testy." As an afterthought, I held out my hand and added, "Please."

I realized it wasn't much of an apology.

Roger looked at my hand for a long moment without moving. I wasn't sure he was going to take it, and I wouldn't have blamed him if he didn't.

When he finally did reach over, his eyes smiled at me, even if the rest of his face remained serious.

"Forgotten," he said, "but I expect you to call me right away if this melancholy of yours becomes any more of a problem. I think we both know why."

I expected him to head off to his own car, but he stood right where he was, silent as a statue, and watched me open my driver's door. Having him continue to stare at me that way made me very uncomfortable.

"Look," I said, exasperated, "I've got it under control." I let go of the handle and started to put my hands on my hips until I realized what a stupid gesture it was.

"Sure you do," Roger said, "but I'm checking with you in the morning anyway."

He turned and got into his car with only one look back. I got into mine and started it a moment later, but waited for Roger to drive away before I put it in gear and headed back to my big, lonely, empty house.

Sure you do.

I heard his words again in my head a short time later, as I drove into my neighborhood, turned down my street, opened the gate and pulled into the long drive that lead to the house.

It was already dark, and all the lights were off except those by the gateposts. I shuddered as I drove up to the front door. I looked at the dark house and didn't want to get out of the car.

As I sat there in driveway, I didn't even want to open the garage to put the car away. Instead, I sat there with my head in my hands and cried.

Sure you do.

He obviously knew me well.

CHAPTER 5

R andy and Janice's wedding should have been a very pleasant diversion. As she walked down the aisle that day, Janice was as beautiful as any bride will ever be. In fact, I distinctly remembered my comment to *Puz* the first morning we ever saw her.

"Is that a babe?" he had asked.

"Yeah," I answered, "that's a babe."

Randy, waiting for her at the altar, had a great big grin on his scarred face. He looked to me like a handsome pirate, right out of a storybook. I began to relax as they exchanged their vows.

It was a good feeling. I knew as I sat there I would have regretted not going. Roger had certainly been right on that score. I thought he had made a very good call getting me to attend. I missed my friends very much.

However, afterward, instead of pleasant memories, we brought home thoughts of the madman *Micah,* who had changed all our worlds yet again. Roger, no doubt sensing the same tightness inside I felt about it, promised to check in on me. Like always, he was as good as his word.

I had learned long ago that I could count on him to do exactly what he said he'd do. My phone rang very early in the morning and he seemed somewhat surprised when I told him I was already up and doing just fine.

To tell the truth, being depressed had become such a natural part of me, so was I. Still, it was hard not to laugh at him when Roger asked me the same inane question for the third time in the space of five minutes.

"Are you *really* all right?"

"Yes, Roger, I'm fine." I grimaced a little and shook my head at the telephone, glad he couldn't see me.

"Are you *sure?*" he said again, his words emphasizing his deep concern for my welfare.

I suppose I can't blame him. My mental state has been suspect ever since I got back from 'Nam. Losing Carrie had unraveled me almost to the point of a second breakdown, as Roger well knew. Back in Brickdale, the thug Micah, and what he tried to do to all of us, was nearly the last straw.

"Honest," I lied, "I'm fine."

I knew he was enough of a friend that saying anything else to him would ring alarm bells, and I didn't want him trying to do something about it.

Besides, at that moment, it wasn't that big a lie. After helping my friends through the insanity with Micah, I honestly thought I'd finally found some measure of peace. I thought about those few moments standing alone with Janice, when I had poured my heart out to her and realized the world wasn't out to get me anymore.

Despite that miserable weekend, my nightmares had all become dormant for a while.

"You certainly didn't look fine last night," Roger said. He kept it up the whole time he was on the phone.

Protecting your pot of gold? It wasn't my most generous thought. "I'll be all right," I said. "You don't need to monitor my behavior...*Mom*." Roger ignored my dig.

I was glad when he finally hung up.

However, he kept his morning check-up running for several more days. His constantly vocalized concern soon began to be upsetting. On the morning of the fifth day I finally got tired of the routine and refused to answer.

My silence must have worried him.

"Are you still there, Paul?"

"Oh, sure...I'm here," I said. I was being deliberately rude to him, pouring all the sarcasm I could muster into my words. "I'm here, Roger. I just hadn't heard you say any goddam thing to me that was *new*...that's all."

There was a protracted silence on his end.

Roger finally laughed, if you could call his sorry little chuckle laughter.

23

"Okay," he said, clearing his throat, "You win. I guess I *am* getting a little old with it. I'm going to call off the search and rescue."

"Oh, is that what you call it?"

He laughed again, a real one this time, and I laughed along with him. At that moment, I really did feel all right, and there was every reason to believe my good spirits would continue.

Unfortunately, it wasn't long after that last call from Roger the memories started to invade my dreams again. At first, they were only occurring a couple of times a week. At least, that's all I could remember, even though I often woke up in a cold sweat. It was only little things, but they got particularly bad when I was alone at night.

That, I think, was the crux of the problem, because I *was* alone, nearly every night, sitting all by myself in that big, empty house.

Before long the nightmares were happening to me again almost every night...and there was nothing dreamlike about any of them. They were realistic and frightening.

Several nights they woke me up, frantic, and on those nights I was afraid to turn off the light and go back to sleep.

At first, I had dreams about my old friend Albert Parker again, laying in his white coffin at McDermott's Funeral Home back in Brickdale.

In my dreams, he never moved or spoke. That wasn't the frightening part. It was the things I'd never taken the time to say to him before he died. They seemed to run like a voiceover in the background, and hearing them made my whole body tremble.

My former war buddy, Blake was soon there again, too. I remember how I once laughed at him in 'Nam, and thought of nicknaming him *Oddball*. In my newest round of night terrors, he was never anything to laugh at. He was always the disturbing stalker he became...*Shadow Man*.

In my dreams, I also relived the horrendous car crash he had caused. Each time I did, I heard Carrie's last words to me all over again.

"Paul, it hurts so much."

It had taken a lot of therapy to get those thoughts out of my head. They started up all over again after my return from the wedding...with one major difference. Now in my dreams Carrie's eyes would snap open after her last breath, and her face would be a mask of hate as she snarled up at me.

"This was all your fault."

I knew there was truth hidden in that accusation. I'll always feel that way, no matter what anyone says.

This was all your fault.

God, how I hated that dream. I would wake up in a cold sweat from the rest of my nightmares...but I'd always wake up crying from that one.

CHAPTER 6

Less than a month after my return from Brickdale the nightmares were back. Albert was there, along with my sweet Carrie...and an endless array of nameless Viet Cong. They became relentless, in a slow, steady march. *Micah* was there, too. It got so bad I couldn't sleep at night, and I lost my appetite.

I tried to hide it from everyone, which is easy to do when you work alone most of the time, but it wasn't long before my clothes all began getting baggy and the dark shadows under my eyes attested to my lack of rest.

I thought I was strong enough to cope with it by myself, but the dreams continued to escalate, getting worse faster than at any time before, until I knew I would have to schedule psychiatric sessions again. It was either that or go insane, a choice that sometimes didn't sound all that bad.

Jim Hammond noticed the changes in my behavior before I said anything. The good doctor and his wife had been our dearest friends in the old Rancho Santa Fe neighborhood. Even though I'd moved to Cielo after Carrie died, they still came by often.

Eleven weeks to the day after I'd returned from Randy and Janice's wedding, Jim and Eva dropped by again, this time totally unannounced.

I didn't think much about it, even though that, all by itself, was strange. They were as straight-laced and Ann Landers proper as they come, and they would usually call before dropping by.

That afternoon they just showed up at the gate.

Of course, I opened it to let them in as soon as I heard their voices on the speaker. I was looking forward to seeing them and welcomed the company. I watched their car come up the drive until it was just outside the front porch. When they came up on the steps I already had the door open.

Once inside, the first thing Jim did was show me a chilled bottle of white wine.

"I've had this in the cooler since yesterday," he said, tapping the bottle, "just so I could open it here with you...so don't you even think of saying no."

Eva smiled her shy-little-girl smile and gave me the quick hug and perfunctory kiss on the cheek everyone in the Rancho Santa Fe area used to greet each other, but Jim, despite his words, didn't even hold out his hand.

Instead, he cocked his head from one side to the other. As he looked at me that way, his right eyebrow shot up with his question.

"Have you been sleeping all right, Paul?"

"Sure," I lied, thinking he'd never notice.

"Well, you look like shit," he muttered.

"Jim!" Eva said, her voice rising, "That's no way to talk to our friend." She slapped her husband's arm. "Where are your manners?"

"It's all right, Eva," I said, plopping down in the nearest chair and sighing, "he's right."

Jim walked over to the bar and fished the opener out of the top drawer. He'd been there so often he knew exactly where it was, in the far-right corner, as if he'd been the one to place it there in the first place. He uncorked his bottle and proceeded to pour three glasses of wine.

"So," he asked, wiping a small drip off the counter and handing me a glass, "What's wrong?"

"Roger's got me crashing on another deadline."

Something about Jim's silence after my statement seemed to crush the air in the room.

"Don't bullshit me," Jim said.

"What?"

"I've never known you to let your agent push you hard for much of anything."

Touché. I tried to smile and failed.

Jim gave his wife a glass of wine and took a slow sip

from his own. He took the seat next to me, sitting on the chair's edge and leaning toward me, never looking away.

They'd either rehearsed their performance, or Eva took his comment and demeanor as her cue to be silent, because she stood beside the piano, looking, one by one, at the many picture arrangements on the lid instead of at us, without saying a word. She didn't even look up.

"It's actually the publisher pushing," I said, looking first at Eva, then at Jim. When I looked back again at Eva, I realized I really couldn't face either one of them with that lie. I finally looked down at my shoes, wishing with all my heart my friends hadn't stopped by that day at all.

"Bullshit," Jim said again. "Something's wrong."

"No," I said, "honest, it's just a miserable deadline, and I have writer's block."

"You're having those nightmares again, aren't you?"

Eva gasped, but Jim remained silent, looking at me. It was me that broke our eye contact.

"Is it really that obvious?" I looked at the two of them, embarrassed. Eva dropped her eyes, but Jim didn't.

"If you recall," Jim said, "You went through something like this before. I saw you that time, too." He hesitated a moment, studying me. "I thought your problem was all over, but I guess it isn't."

"How did you know?"

"You mean, besides the shitty way you look?"

"Jim!"

"Actually," Jim said, ignoring his wife, "Roger Craig called me. He thought I should visit you after that fiasco you went through back in Brickdale."

"Roger told you about that?"

"It took him a while to get it all out but, yes, he did...every bit of it," Jim said, looking up at his wife. "He told us he was worried about you, but I think he needed to get it off his chest, too."

"He did seem to be awfully concerned," Eva said in a whisper, "and I don't blame him. It sounded dreadful." She stood there beside the piano wringing her hands together, while Jim sat stoically and watched my eyes.

Jim must have seen the concern on my face. "I'm not violating Roger's confidentiality, Paul. He's not a patient. He was talking to us as a friend...one very worried about you."

"The *Dodger* has been through a lot with me," I said, using my nickname for Roger. "Even more than the two of you." I felt like crying, but laughed, in spite of myself, and looked back and forth at them.

Jim just stared at me, and Eva looked puzzled, as if she hadn't totally understood my reference. I realized she knew a lot of what had happened from Roger's confessions, but some earlier things I had told to Jim, as my doctor, so she didn't have a clue.

"Paul," Jim started to say, "you don't have to..."

"It's all right," I said. "Two crazy stalkers in a lifetime is quite enough for anyone, don't you think?"

I was trying to be silly, but Jim didn't laugh. "Paul, you don't have to talk about it now," he said as he stood up. "This is not the right time or place." He looked at his wife, closed his eyes and sighed. "Come to my office tomorrow. My first appointment isn't until ten o'clock, so come before nine. I'll make time. We can talk all about it then."

As he walked to the door, I grunted, but when I didn't answer right away in words, he stopped. He put his hands on the back of a chair and stood there looking at me.

"That *is* all right with you, isn't it Paul?"

"Yeah, sure." I nodded my agreement and watched as Jim gently put his hand on the small of Eva's back to guide her toward the front door.

"Tomorrow at nine," he turned and said again.

"I'll be there," I promised.

"I'll be back to get you," he said, fixing me with a hard stare, "if you're not."

Watching the two of them leave, I thought again of Carrie. The two of us had stood together many times, hand-in-hand, in our Rancho Santa Fe house, watching Jim and Eva walk out to their car. My house was different now, but it felt like a familiar sight to me, only now I stood alone, watching in silence as the two of them left.

I had to stop myself from reaching instinctively for Carrie's hand. Instead, I watched from the front door, biting my lower lip as the two of them drove out the long drive and through the opening gate. I watched until their car disappeared beyond the hedge just outside the entrance and the gate closed behind them.

None of us bothered to wave.

CHAPTER 7

When I walked into Jim's pristine inner office the following morning, the first thing I asked him was what kind of happy pill he was going to give me. "You have no idea the number of things I need to forget this time," I joked.

I was only trying to lighten the mood, and bring a semblance of a smile to the scowl on his face, but Jim didn't seem to think my reference was as funny as I did.

"Psychotherapy is treating depression by talking about the causes of your condition and any related issues, not medicating yourself into numbness," he said.

"C'mon, Jim," I said, "Lighten up. Isn't it standard?"

"No," he said, almost snapping at me, "I don't want to get you started on medication. We didn't do it before, and we're not going to do it now. It won't be good for you."

His face remained pleasant but there was a note of anger in his voice.

I was a little bit surprised, but I suppose I should have expected it. As long as I've known him, Jim has never minced words and he probably never will. I realized as I looked at him that I liked him for that.

"So, we're just going to sit and talk?" I crossed my legs and leaned back on the couch. "Couldn't we do that in a restaurant...or a nice, cozy bar booth, where I could at least order us a drink to numb things a bit?" At that moment, numbness actually didn't sound so bad to me.

I heard volumes in the deep breath Jim took before he spoke. "You know damned well it doesn't work that way," he said, leaning forward in his chair. "I've told you before."

Here comes the posturing, I thought.

"You're the doc," I said.

Jim exhaled slowly and seemed to carefully consider each of his next words. I wondered if it was an affectation, or a behavior he learned in medical school.

"Different types of psychotherapy can be effective for treating depression," he said, enunciating each word like he was a prophet dispensing the Lord's wisdom. "Talking about it can help you adjust to a particular crisis, find ways to cope with it and...perhaps...solve future problems."

"Go for it," I said, which I'm sure wasn't really the wholehearted endorsement he wanted. I'd been through a lot of conversations since 'Nam similar to where this one seemed to be headed, and I wasn't overly impressed. I may joke about it or make light of it now, but I have to admit Jim Hammond was extremely good at his business. He'd proven it with me once already.

"You asked for it," was all he said.

He caught my attention as soon as he started talking and he held onto it every moment, despite my decidedly lackluster commitment. But he was unsparing and relentless and that first session couldn't end fast enough for me.

The regular sessions with him that followed were just short of brutal. I saw him twice a week for the first month, and once a week thereafter. Before six months had passed I realized I was sleeping through the night.

Within a year, he had helped me to overcome most of the nightmares. With very few exceptions, I was not only sleeping at night, but the words had started to flow again, much to the delight of Roger and my publisher.

My new book was a thriller, set in a neighborhood a lot like the place where I grew up. It was a natural extension of the other books I'd written and, once the block was gone...thanks to Jim...the words seemed to put themselves down on the paper all by themselves.

As my agent, Roger was smiling a lot now. My writing was going well again, and my mind was at peace. I even started to make some brand-new friends in my Cielo neighborhood. Looking back on it now, it seems obvious it wasn't something that would last.

CHAPTER 8

Unfortunately, my writing starting to go well again was overshadowed by the beginning of a different kind of trouble. The publisher, for some obscure reason, thought it would help to sell my next book if they tried to capitalize on the things that had happened in what they had decided to call *the Brickdale Incident*.

I fully understood the concept of earned media. It was really just another term for word-of-mouth advertising. Marketing agencies and publishers all routinely pitch their supposedly uncanny ability to generate it for their clients. I knew mine did, too. I guess I never realized how far they would go to accomplish it.

I was deep into my new manuscript again when, totally by chance, I saw the first trumped-up article. I'd run out to pick up a few groceries and a bottle of wine when I saw the headline in one of those sleazy tabloids in the racks beside the supermarket checkout.

It was an article complete with a dark, grainy image of the carnage outside the reception hall, obtained from some poor fool at Randy and Janice's wedding. The clerk looked at me when I bought it and shook her head. It was a small gesture I'm sure she meant for herself. *You never know who's going to read all that trashy shit, do you?*

I bought it anyway, and read the article in the parking lot. As I feared, it detailed the insanity that had happened at Randy's wedding.

However, I think what infuriated me the most, there was far too much in it specifically about me and my books, including information on a book that was still in the edit phase. It was far too much information for it to be happenstance. I was certain it was the publisher who had planted the story without my knowledge or permission.

Earned media. Anything to sell books.

Livid, I called Roger and asked him to meet me at the publisher's office. I wouldn't tell him why. I waited in the outer office, while the receptionist eyed my nervous pacing.

The moment Roger arrived I stormed into the publicist's office ahead of him, without waiting to be announced.

"How dare you!" I shouted, waving the supermarket tabloid over my head like a flag. Normally, I got along just fine with the publicist, Ben Lilly, but the poor man was the first person I saw, so he took the full brunt of my anger.

"What...?" he said, surprised.

"You have no right to involve my friends in this, damn it," I screamed at him, shaking the tabloid right under his nose. "No right at all."

If I hadn't been so angry I could easily have seen poor Ben didn't have a clue what my rampage was about. He stammered a response and backpedalled his way into his own supervisor's office. I followed him, knocking over a stack of books and papers in my haste. I almost smacked poor Roger's face with the door as I slammed it.

"What's the meaning of releasing this bullshit?"

I have to give him credit. Ben's supervisor leaned back in his high-backed chair and listened to my harangue without interrupting. When I finished, he leaned forward with both elbows on his desk.

"If you'd like me to have someone in legal contact you, I'll arrange it," he said, "but we have total discretion in how we advertise your work. *Total.* You have no say in it. It's in your contract."

He looked so smug I wanted to punch him.

"You have no right," I repeated.

"It's in the contract of *all* our writers," he said. "You signed it. I suggest you might want to read it."

I was so close to physical blows I probably would have hit the man, if Roger hadn't restrained me.

"He's right, Paul," Roger said, grabbing my upper arm, "it's standard contract language."

"It's totally unacceptable," I said, fuming, "My friends are off limits." I tried to stare daggers at the man. "You got that? They didn't sign your fucking contract. I suggest you consider all of them a *no-fly* zone."

"I repeat," he said, "the publishing company has full discretion on all advertising and promotion for your work." He leaned back in his leather swivel chair.

Unbelievably, he reached into the carved humidifier on his desk, took out a huge cigar, cut the end off and picked up the fancy etched brass lighter that sat next to the box. "So, we'll tell *you* what's acceptable and what isn't," he said, flicking the flame to life.

He lit the cigar and, with a grand gesture, sent a rude plume of smoke in my direction.

"I want that whole section struck from the contract," I said. "My friends are not to be dragged through shit, just so you can make a few more dollars."

"You seem to forget...you make money, too," he said as he blew another ill-mannered plume of smoke at me.

"Change it," I said, "now."

"The contract stands, Mister Barrett."

"Did you hear what I said?" I was shouting.

He tapped the ash from his cigar. "As I told you," he said, folding his arms across his chest, "*we* will decide what's acceptable to advertise and what isn't. All you have to do is write."

"That's all you have to say?" I said, incredulous.

"That's it," he said, looking smug and self-righteous.

"Then, *William*," I said, reading the name etched on the brass nameplate over the words *Advertising Director* in the center of his desk, "I suggest you go fuck yourself. Find someone else to write this shit for you...I'm done."

Ben Lilly and Roger just stood there dumbfounded.

"I doubt that very much, Mr. Barrett," Bill Tomey said, picking up his cigar again and clenching it in his teeth. "It's an ironclad contract."

"We'll see about that," I said.

"Yes," Bill said, picking up his phone, "we will." His eyes were cold. "You'll write for us, Barrett, or you may not write for *anyone*."

Sadly, he was right.

CHAPTER 9

Even though I swore I wasn't going to put down another word, my writing pace actually doubled. Just to keep things straight, however, it wasn't something I was doing for the publisher. I was doing it entirely to keep myself sane.

After I stormed out of Bill Tomey's office, I took my complaint to the publisher's review committee, and they...surprise, surprise...unanimously agreed with their obnoxious ad director. Their response upset me so much, I said some really nasty things about planting Janice's wedding disaster in those sleazy tabloid pages for publicity. I told them no matter what lawsuits they threatened, I was *really* through writing for them, contract or no contract.

They pretty much ignored me, until I leaked the whole sordid story to the press. They took *that* like I expected they would. They're all for publicity of any kind for the author, but they don't like bad publicity for themselves. It makes their stock price drop.

They stopped every bit of advertising for my books and demanded the immediate return of my last advance. All of it that hadn't already been earned back through sales, anyway. They were also adamant about holding me to a five-year non-compete clause...something else buried deep in the *blah-blah* rhetoric of their multiple-page ring-binder-filling contract language.

Roger and my lawyers got them to agree to a two-year non-compete term, instead. Either way would have been fine with me. I had sold so many books I had enough stashed away in my bank accounts to live comfortably for several years without writing another word.

For the stipulated period, I couldn't sell new stories to anyone else. Of course, they didn't have to promote me anymore either, if I wasn't writing for them. But the judge decreed they *did* have to continue to pay all the royalties due for any books sold.

They tried to get my books back from the retailers that were stocking them, but they were selling so well most of the retailers were slow to return them. The retailers made more on each sale than I did, but my old publisher was the one who had to cut the royalty check to me every quarter.

I had to smile. Even without advertising support, my books still sold extremely well, and with each sale I was drawing a royalty they couldn't deny to me. I could live for years on that alone.

I think that rankled them the most.

To top it all, good old Roger had paperwork done and ready for me to sign with one of their major competitors the day after I left.

I signed the end-of-contract agreement one afternoon and went across town with Roger the following morning to sign with the new publisher. They were only too happy to have me, even if they couldn't sell anything I wrote for at least two years. We both knew it would take a while to get anything into print anyway, even if I had a manuscript complete, edited and set in type.

The old publisher made all kinds of threatening noises about my new signing, but there was little they could actually do. Before the waiting period was over, I re-took control of *all* my books. Roger had from the first seen to it that I retained all reprint rights.

I had some concerns they would try to besmirch my reputation when I left, but Roger said that often backfired and generated more publicity that would continue to sell the existing books...and earn royalties they had to pay, so they would keep silent. He was right again.

At that point...hell, I just didn't care.

Before all the shit started, I'd made up my mind to find time to write every day...for at least a few hours. I realized a long time ago I didn't write for sales, money, nor acclaim.

I kept writing because I had stories to tell.

It was often a labor that lasted all day long and well into the night. Plus, it kept my mind off other things and made the weeks pass faster.

With or without a publisher, I'd reached a point in my life where I was *compelled* to write. When I put my mind to it, the words poured out of me so fast they seemed at times almost unstoppable.

The good thing about being so possessed, it kept my mind off just about everything else.

The two-year non-compete arrangement was history before I really had any time to think about it. My new publishers held a party in their office to celebrate when the start date of our arrangement arrived. There was a lot of hand-shaking and photography to go along with the plastic glasses of champagne. Their publicity machine was set in motion, big time, to advertise the new contract.

Of course, it meant a lot of running around, for me, schmoozing for the publishing tabloids and reviewers. The appointment calendar was full for another full year. I went along with it, because it was expected of me, but thought of it like having to hold my breath under water.

It was something I had to do to survive, even though I didn't care one whit about any of it.

I just wanted to write. I had already been writing every single day of the week, seldom missing a day, every week of the past year. By the afternoon of the party I was not only done with the manuscript they expected, I had a second novel almost done and ready to go to edit, and there hadn't been any pressure from anywhere, except from myself.

I desperately wanted to finish that second story, too, because I had an idea for yet another one already brewing in the back of my head. That third story was nagging me to get it started, so I was crunching on the second one like there was a deadline of yesterday.

The new publisher was ecstatic.

CHAPTER 10

I was writing the final chapter of that second new story when the nagging squeal of a passing emergency siren startled me out of deep concentration. It was such an unusual sound in my neighborhood I jumped when I heard it and knocked my cup off the desk.

I felt my coffee, which had long ago grown cold, splash over the front of my legs. The sound of the cup smashing itself into tiny pieces on the tile floor a heartbeat later seemed unbelievably loud.

Give it up, Barrett. You don't have to make any damn fool deadline. Remember?

I sat up, stretched and tried to ignore the cold, dark liquid dripping off my lap, as the wail of the siren that had wakened me from my reverie faded in the distance. The vertebrae in my back responded to my stretch with a series of subtle pops. I rolled my head from side-to-side and felt the crackling continue. It actually felt pretty good.

Putting my arms up over my head further eased the ache in my neck, but that's when I made the mistake of glancing at the clock that ticked quietly beside me.

Eight o'clock. Where did the day go?

I found it hard to believe I'd been sitting at the desk for almost eleven unbroken hours without typing the words I had been so furiously racing toward.

The End.

I rubbed my eyes. They felt like they were full of sand, and it took a great effort to stifle my sudden urge to yawn. When I stood up a moment later, the knots in the muscles of my calves and lower back told me I'd been hunched over the keyboard far too long. One look into the small mirror I kept on my desk confirmed the worst of my suspicions.

Jeez...Hammond was right...you still look like shit.

Even though I'd gained back some weight, whenever he saw me, Jim Hammond made a point of chiding me all over again for the way I looked. My constantly bedraggled appearance was apparently okay when it was something caused by the relentless push of a creative spirit, instead of some insidious nightmare.

I was barefoot, so I tried to avoid the pieces of the broken cup in the spreading coffee puddle on the floor and stumbled into the kitchen, hoping to find the housekeeper. I fully intended to clean up my own mess, but that was not the reason I sought her out. At that moment, more than anything else, I wanted to hear another human voice...even though I realized it was unlikely at this hour for Jasmine to still be there. The sun was going down and the rooms were starting to get dark. She would have gone home hours ago.

When the phone rang announcing someone at the gate it startled me. I thought I was about to get my wish for human contact, but it was only a car from the San Diego County sheriff, checking on the rumor of a disturbance in the area.

"Sir, I'm officer Johns with the San Diego County Sheriff's office," he said over the speaker. "Have you seen or heard anything suspicious this evening?"

"Not a sound out here for hours," I said, "except a siren a few moments ago."

"You probably heard the siren as we approached the area. May I ask you to identify yourself?"

When I told him my name I could hear someone in the background say *That checks.*

"What's going on, officer? Is there a problem?"

"Someone called to report a disturbance in this area," Officer Johns, said. "You're sure you haven't heard anything unusual this evening?"

"Just your siren."

He apologized for bothering me and hung up.

As I stood in the clean, empty kitchen, wondering what was going on outside, my stomach started rumbling.

I rummaged around in the refrigerator until I discovered the other thing I had been secretly hoping to find. A sandwich left for me on a covered plate.

Thank you, Jasmine.

By the lengthening shadows in the valley, I knew the sun was about to disappear below the horizon. It's a simple daily fact that doesn't sound like much to most people, but after all that's happened to me, I find it difficult, if not impossible, to suppress a heavy shudder after sunset. At least when I'm home alone.

Which I usually am.

It isn't that I'm afraid of the dark. Far from it.

After all the shit I've seen in my life, there's very little running around in the night anymore that scares me. Still, most of us are surrounded by ghosts we have to learn to live with, and I'm no different.

Death and dying are not a lot of fun to see. I'd seen so much of it the memories are sometimes a lot to cart around, even though I don't have to visit Jim Hammond on a professional basis any more.

At least not regularly.

Once in a while...when it gets particularly tough for me to take a breath...I drop in on him without an appointment and bend his ear for a while.

He's usually pretty good about it.

Having conquered all those ghosts, or at least learning how to keep them at bay, the mere fact of the sun going down for the night doesn't scare me at all. I just don't like the heightened feeling of being alone again the darkness brings along with it.

That's why it became part of my routine each night to wander from room-to-room and turn on as many lights as I could. I also made sure all the outside lights were flipped on as I passed their switches. People who have witnessed my nightly ritual have filled the tabloids with stories of my phobia, but none of them ever get it right. I'm not afraid of the dark. I simply hate the bone-crushing silence.

I saw the Sheriff's car drive away from my gate, then sat alone at the little table in my kitchen, watching the sky outside grow darker with a feeling of dread, not certain I really wanted the sandwich after all.

I had to suppress a shudder. Even with all the lights on, the depressing loneliness of the house at night still bothers me. It makes me wonder why I had been so adamant about privacy in the first place. Sitting by myself, watching *Cheers* on television did little to ease the empty feeling of the place.

CHAPTER 11

Ordinarily, I would have gone out and run through my regular time-wasting liturgy, which included flitting from some of the nearby tony restaurants to some of the less raunchy bars. I didn't drink. Not much anyway. I didn't want to get that kind of routine started.

I'd usually just wander in, say hello to the bartenders in each place, most of whom knew me all too well by now, and leave. I'd often wind up simply drinking coffee and chatting with other patrons to pass the time. There weren't any real friends anywhere, but that was fine. I didn't recognize many of the people who said hello, but I was happy to talk to them anyway. I just wanted company.

I deliberated making the rounds again tonight, but I was tired. For a moment, I even thought about calling Roger Craig, but decided not to bother him. He was a good friend, but it was hard for him not to slip into the "literary agent" role when we talked.

I could have used the company, but I hated the thought of spending my time talking about publishing contracts and manuscript deadlines, when all I really wanted was to hear another human voice to keep the memory of all those ghosts in my nightmares at bay.

I glanced at the framed eight-by-ten glossy photo on the piano, and memories of *The Twins*, Janice, *Puz* and a younger me...*the old Reichold Street gang*...as I often thought of the bunch of us, flooded over me.

They were good memories that made me smile.

I also felt a pang of deep regret about not talking to any of them in such a long time. The picture had been taken in Brickdale, at Randy and Janice's wedding, the last time we'd all been together, almost three years ago.

Every time I looked at it, I was reminded of the awful strain of that meeting, interrupted as it was by that crazed madman. The picture had been taken just before Randy and Janice's "first dance." Mere minutes before that lunatic appeared at their reception. I thought that, at least, had been fortunate. Otherwise, the panic of that night could have shown in everyone's eyes, and the portrait would have become a picture I didn't want to look at as often as I did. I didn't imagine anyone would.

As I picked up the framed print and held it, I realized how long it had been since I had seen any of my old friends.

It had been almost as long since I had spoken to them on the phone. I'd kept tabs on them, in a way. Roger came by or called at least three times a week and he told me about the success Don Camron was starting to have with his short-story collections.

The last time he called, he told me how Donnie's brother Randy had just written a very good memoir about his service time in the Navy. He thought they were both so good he was representing both of them now.

"Don Camron is selling well and Randy's memoir has *New York Times* bestseller written all over it," Roger had gushed when he told me. "You Brickdale boys are really something else."

Sadly, although I talked to Roger often, I never called either one of *The Twins* to congratulate them. *Too busy* was my mantra to myself, when the real reason had more to do with avoiding old memories. I was ashamed of myself for having neglected them for so long.

You're an arrogant fool, Barrett.

I don't know why the forced solitude of my house that particular night seemed more intense than usual. Maybe it was the weariness that seemed to emanate from my every pore after driving myself so relentlessly, but I realized I missed all those guys more than I cared to admit.

My time on Reichold Street often felt like it had been three lifetimes ago, but that group represented the closest friends I'd ever known and, in the quiet of that evening I thought it would be nice to talk to them again.

I almost called them, then and there. I even had my hand on the receiver, until I glanced at the clock again and realized it was well after nine o'clock...closer to ten. That meant it would be almost one in the morning back east.

Most phone calls received in the wee hours are not usually made to tell you anything good, so calling any of them so late at night was sure to be upsetting. I took my hand away from the telephone and decided to make my calls early the next morning instead.

As it turned out, I didn't have to...and as I think back on it now, it was another one of the pivotal life events we don't think much of at the time, even though they sometimes seem to forever alter the future. That particular night, however, there wasn't any good or bad associated with it at all. It was just a simple decision that let me relax enough go to sleep.

CHAPTER 12 - Janice

The book-signing tour Roger described to my Randy didn't sound very exciting to me, but then it wasn't *my* book being sold. To me, it amounted to a lot of sitting around, trying not to look far too hopeful, just waiting for people to show up...and that was at each venue he mentioned. I couldn't see how either one of them would be interested in that part of it.

I thought about going with Randy and his brother, since it was going to be for several weeks in southern California, but we had been to that area several years ago, when we all endured that awful loony who had been stalking Paulie.

I used to think we were a pretty tight group. After that awful character at Paulie's, and the doper bastard who tried to kill us at our wedding, I started thinking of the whole bunch of us differently than I used to.

Not so special. More like cursed.

Quite frankly, I wasn't looking forward to going to California again, no matter how much I wanted to see Paul. Roger said there would be nice dinners and maybe a party or two, but the perks weren't all that exciting to me. Particularly not if it meant sitting around all day in the corner of a crowded bookstore, in a town where I knew nobody at all, to earn them.

Other than Roger, Paulie was the only one out there I knew, and he hadn't bothered to call us since the wedding.

I love Randy, and I'm proud of him, but the signing events sounded boring. I hated to tell him I didn't want to go. In fact, I tried to avoid answering him at all, but he kept pushing, and started making noises about having Roger arrange it, so I finally had to admit how I felt.

"Why don't just you and your brother go?"

Randy had been so pumped up about it I was trying not to sound negative about the whole thing.

"You don't want to come?" he said, surprised.

"I'm sorry, hon, it just doesn't sound like fun to me."

"Are you sure?"

When Randy had started writing, he was surprisingly good at telling stories about his time in the Navy. I don't usually like war-related stuff, because it always reminds me of my late step-brother Albert. But Randy's book was really interesting and I enjoyed reading it. I really did. Just not enough to sit around in a place where whispering was frowned upon, planted on hard chairs...perhaps for weeks...in a series of bookstores, trying to sell his book to people who might not give a damn.

"I'm sure," I said. He looked so crestfallen I had to go over and hug him.

"You're *really* sure?" he said.

"It will be a good chance for you and your brother to bond again," I said as I wrapped my arms around him.

"I'd like that, Randy smiled.

"I know," I said as I hugged him. Donnie had been doing so well he almost seemed like his old self, and it was his success with his collection of short stories that got Randy interested in writing his memoir in the first place.

"You *really* don't want to come?" Randy said again, looking like a little boy who has just been scolded.

"As much as I love you, husband dear," I said, "it sounds boring as hell." I kissed him on the cheek to try and soften the blow.

Randy laughed. "We could stop off in Vegas before we come home," he said, "just you and me. We could get one of those rooms with mirrors on the ceiling." He winked at me with that scarred, yet little boy face of his.

"No offense, Love," I said, "but Vegas doesn't appeal to me in the slightest...with or without mirrors."

"If you're sure." Randy looked so much like a sad little puppy when he said it I wanted to laugh.

"I'm sure," I said, putting on my serious face for him.

"You two go out to the coast, sell some books and have a good time. I'll be fine." I thought that was the end of it.

When their three-week tour was over, I was supposed to pick them both up at the Capitol City airport. It was the first time since we'd been married that we'd spent so much time apart. Randy called me every day to tell me how things were going...and to say he loved me.

I liked that part.

However, the day they were supposed to return, Randy surprised me. I thought he was calling to confirm their flight number and arrival time, but his call was to tell me Donnie was coming home alone.

"Alone?" Why aren't you coming, too?"

"Well," he said, stuttering a little, "I th-thought I'd make a stop in Las Vegas."

"*Vegas*, Randy?"

"We talked about it," he said, "remember?"

"I know, but..." It was all I got a chance to say.

"Everybody says how neat it is," he said. "I really want to be able to say I've seen it, too...that I've been there at least once, ya know?"

"You're not getting a room with mirrors without me, are you?" I teased.

He sounded hurt when he answered. "Of course not, Jannie," he said. "I just wanted to see the casinos and maybe take in a show or two. I don't know when I'll ever be this close again."

He sounded just like my little brother Kevin, begging for ice cream and cake.

"Well..." I said, in a tone sure to tease him.

"I only plan to be there the one day, Jan. I can call you later with my return flight info."

"I guess it's all right," I said. "Just *one* day?"

There was a long pause.

"If it takes longer than I think and I need to get a room," Randy said, "it'll be in one of the cheaper mom-and-pop places off the Strip, not the expensive clubs."

"So, you don't know when you're coming home?"

"No, Jan, I...uh..." he stuttered.

He always stuttered when he was nervous.

I knew he wanted to take in a show and visit the casino. He was trying to cram a lot into the time he had but, no matter when he started, I'm sure he also knew he'd have to stay overnight. He didn't want to tell me that, and he couldn't keep a secret to save his life.

"I was just teasing, silly," I said. "Go have fun, you earned it. Are you sure Donnie will be all right heading back here all by himself? I know he's been doing lots better lately, but..."

"He'll be fine, Jan," Randy said, interrupting me. "I don't think he'll have any problem at all."

"Well," I teased again, "as long as it's only a day or two...and no rooms with mirrors." I waited for several moments before I heard his answer.

"I promise," Randy said, "and I'll call you with my return flight info as soon as I have it." His relief at my acquiescence was evident.

"You'd better, Mister," I said and blew him a kiss.

I didn't tell him the other reason I was so agreeable. I'd received a letter the afternoon before from the brother of one of the men my step-brother, Albert, had saved in Vietnam. My step-mother, Anna, had forwarded it to me. His name was Jimmy Lewis.

I remembered when his brother had showed up in his uniform at Albert's funeral. His letter told me his brother had seemed fine, once fully healed from his wounds, but he couldn't ever seem to hold a job.

Jimmy said his brother tried going back to school, but dropped out. He couldn't concentrate. He worked for a while pumping gas, then as a car wash attendant. The letter covered several hand-written pages as he told me how his brother had started to fall apart, and bounced around from indifference to anger to guilt.

"He had a lot of guilt about simply being alive," Jimmy wrote, "when so many of his friends had died."

Jimmy ended the letter by telling me how his brother had hanged himself in the locker room of the school where he'd just been hired as a janitor. That by itself was enough to make me cry, but it was the last line of his letter that really tore me up.

I thought you'd want to know.

I suppose it was his way of coping with what had finally happened to his brother. As if sharing that hurt was going to somehow make it any easier. I suppose it did...for him. God knows I've been there. I couldn't help wondering when it would all end.

I didn't have the heart to shove so much negativity on Randy, when he seemed so happy and excited. I wanted to keep him that way...happy.

Donnie came home later that night as planned, and I picked him up at the airport. Randy was right about him. He'd had no travel problems at all. He chattered about the trip and the people he'd met all the way home.

He sounded so sure of himself again I knew my decision to let his brother fulfill an item on his own bucket list was the right thing to do. *The old Donnie is back.* What a neat feeling that was. It made me forget, for a moment, that awful letter.

"What was the best part about the book tour," I asked when we were finally in his driveway.

He stepped out of the car and looked around with a really serious look on his face. The way he acted, I thought at first he might have forgotten he had his own place and wasn't staying with us anymore.

"I suppose it was having all those people say such nice things about my writing," he said. He paused for several moments before he went on. "So many people paid me compliments. So many...but you know, Janice," a confused expression overtook his countenance, "there were times it almost seemed like something that had already happened to me...a long time ago."

I couldn't hide my gasp.

"You know, don't you?" he said, cocking his head a little to the side to look at me. "What it was, I mean. I try to remember details about it...but they keep slipping away."

"You were such a good writer," I said, hoping he would let it go at that. "Randy was always so proud of you."

"I'm going to make all of you proud of me," he said as he put Randy's suitcase in the front seat so I wouldn't forget it when I got home.

"You don't have to prove anything, Donnie." I slipped my arm in his and leaned my head on his shoulder.

"Only to myself," he said.

CHAPTER 13 - Donnie

When our book signing tour was just about over, my brother and I were exhausted. At least I was ready to crash. Randy was still so pumped about the whole thing it often seemed like he was ready to race around the block.

"Ya did good, Little Brother," Randy said. "Held your own with a lot of different people, sold some books...and I think you really made a name for yourself. I was proud of you. Roger said he'd send copies of any articles they write."

"You didn't do so bad yourself, Big Brother," I laughed. "That ugly puss of yours didn't seem to scare away too many customers." I was tired, but I hadn't felt so good about things in general in a long time.

"I'm glad it's over," Randy said.

"Me, too. I'm ready to go home."

Randy got a funny look on his face when I said that. "About the trip home..." he said.

At first, I thought Roger, or the publisher, was going to make some unreasonable demand for more of our time. I was shaking my head before Randy finished his thought.

"I'm going home," I said. "I need a rest."

"It isn't more work," Randy said, "it would be more like a vacation."

"A vacation? Randy, we've been away for weeks. I just want to go home."

"I've been looking at charter flights to Vegas," Randy said. It seemed like he was ignoring me, which I didn't like. "Thought we could stop over for a day, just to see the place...we're so close."

"That's not how I want to see Las Vegas," I said. "Blowing in and out like that doesn't seem like any fun to me at all. Not one bit."

"C'mon," Randy said, "it'll be special. Just you and me in the *City That Never Sleeps*."

"That's Chicago, asshole," I said.

"Okay, wise guy," Randy said, frowning, "I meant to say *The City of Lights*."

I said the words right along with him.

"Don't do that," he said.

I smiled at him, but he didn't smile back like he usually did whenever I earned *The Twins* nickname Paulie had given us.

His lips were set in a hard line, and he crossed his arms like he usually did when he was pissed, but my mind was made up.

"I just want to go home, Randy."

Randy looked at me for a long time, and I thought he was going to start an argument until he answered.

"Okay," he said, which surprised me. He said the word with a big sigh. "You go home...but I'm going to Vegas."

"Go home...by myself?" I said. I was a little worried. I honestly couldn't remember the last time I'd gone that kind of distance alone. I knew I *had* done it before...it had just been a long time.

"Why not?" Randy said. He looked like he was trying to smile, but wasn't doing a good job of it.

"Why not?" I repeated. My mind was racing with all the possible things that could go wrong but, in the end, a shrug was all I could come up with. "I don't know," I said.

"You can you get to the airport, can't you?"

"Sure," I said, "I know how to call a cab."

"Will you be able to find your way alone through the airport concourse?"

"I can read the signs, Big Brother."

"Will you know when you've landed back at Capitol City?" Randy said.

"Of course I will, they announce it, silly."

"Then go," Randy said.

"You mean it?" I was more than a little nervous.

"Sure," Randy said. "You'll be fine. I'll call Janice and have her pick you up when you get home, so you won't even have to worry about hailing a cab." He patted me on the shoulder. "You'll be fine. It's about time you started doing things on your own again."

"I wish you'd come home, too," I said.

"This stopover is something I already cleared with Janice," Randy said. "She knows how much I want to see Vegas, and she told me to go ahead, since I'm so close."

"I don't know," I said.

"You sure you don't want to come with me?"

Randy seemed so excited I wanted to acquiesce, but I couldn't find it in me to match his enthusiasm.

"I'm positive," I said.

"Then it's settled." Randy took a deep breath and put his arm across my shoulders. "You're going back home to Brickdale...and I'm going to Vegas for a day."

"I still don't like it," I said, with as serious a face as I could muster.

"You'll be fine," Randy said.

"It isn't me I'm worried about."

"What?" Randy's face actually looked shocked. "You're worried about *me*?"

"You always did get your ass into trouble without me."

He looked confused until I gave him a big smile, and then he stepped close and hugged me.

"I love you, Little Brother," he said.

CHAPTER 14 - Randy

I felt a little funny letting Donnie go home alone, but I was pretty sure he could handle it. He hadn't had any real episodes in such a long time, I couldn't remember the last one. Still, I worried about him. I don't suppose you ever stop worrying about someone you care about.

Roger Craig had been representing Donnie and his short stories, quite successfully, for more than a year. When I finally wrote my memoir, he took one look at it and signed me to a contract, too. He found a publisher by summer.

Once the promotions for my book started, the two of us went everywhere together. The publisher thought it was a great way to attract all kinds of new readers. To say it was anything but a whirlwind would be lying.

Roger met us when we flew out to San Diego for a joint book-signing tour. The tour arrangements had us together all day long, almost every day. In some ways, it was a circus. *Introducing the Camron Brothers.*

As usual, I spent an inordinate amount of my time worrying about my brother, but he was doing so well I decided to make a stop in Las Vegas, rather than return directly home to Brickdale.

"I've even cleared it with Janice," I said to Donnie. "It's the one place she's absolutely *never* wanted to go, but she said I should go see it, as long as I'm so close."

"Then go for it," Donnie said.

"Want to come with me?" I knew he was going to be against the idea, just like Janice had been.

Donnie rolled his eyes, took a deep breath and gave me his *no way* sigh. No amount of talking or pleading could convince him to go with me.

"I'm worn out, Randy. I can't wait to get home."

"You're sure?" I said.

"Why are you so adamant about me coming along?" Donnie said. "You're the one with the great-looking wife waiting for him."

"I didn't think you noticed girls," I laughed.

"Oh, c'mon. I may have some memory issues, but I'm a long way from dead, Mister Camron." He called me *Mister* and poked me on the shoulder, ribbing me just like he used to when we were kids.

"You're sure you'll be all right?"

"Go ahead, Big Brother," Donnie said, "I'll be fine."

His enormous smile when he said it convinced me he would be okay traveling alone this time. I'd spent enough time watching over him. It was time to let him go.

Got to let him live his life.

Still, I made my stopover arrangements for after he was on his way to the airport, and told him it was just so I could be there to say goodbye. He was a bit put out with me.

"I may be your little brother," he said, "but I'm all grown up now, just in case you hadn't noticed. You don't have to hold my hand anymore."

"I don't mind driving you to the airport," I said.

"You didn't think I could call a cab?"

"It's not that, Donnie...I just wanted to help."

"I understand," he said, glancing out the window, "but sometimes you overdo it. I'm not an invalid."

"I know..." I started to say something else, but didn't finish. The look on his face was sour enough to tell me I'd best shut up and let things go.

I knew he was pissed, because Donnie opened his door before I was fully stopped, and he didn't even say goodbye when he got out of the car. I was only taking a carry-on with me to Vegas, so he took my large suitcase and bag of books with him. He gave me one more surly look over his shoulder as he headed to the doors.

I watched as he walked into the terminal until I couldn't see him anymore. Then I headed for the small airport across town where the charter flights hailed from.

The charter company took care of my rental car, and to take my mind off my brother I chatted with the three men who were walking with me out of the old hanger to get on the small plane to Vegas. As we walked, I glanced at my wristwatch. By now, Donnie had been in the air for over three hours. He was almost home.

"You fly over to Vegas often?" I said to the tall red-headed fellow next to me, pointing at the little single engine Cessna Helio Courier sitting outside the hanger.

"Every time there's someone with a charter," he said, smiling. "Name's Mango. I'm you're pilot."

"Mango?" I said, smiling back at him.

"Charlie Mange, actually," he said, "but everybody around here knows me as Mango." He ran his fingers through his mass of yellow-orange curls. "Must be the hair. Whattaya think?"

"Must be." I thought of Paulie calling me and my brother *The Twins*, and had to smile. "Guess I'm lucky mangos aren't popular back home," I said, pointing at my own curly flame-red locks, "although I did have a few guys in the service who used to call me 'Mater."

"If you can call *that* luck," Mango smiled, and I'm sure my face got almost as red as my hair.

"Hey, Mango," said the beefy guy walking behind us, "you still takin' off in that thing tonight? Everybody tells me that damn Cessna is sensitive to crosswinds, and it sure feels windy out here tonight."

"I've taken off in worse," Mango said, losing his smile for a moment. "You want to back out or something?"

"Just wanna be sure I get there," *Beefy* said, patting the valise he carried, "got a big game of baccarat waiting for me tonight."

"That shouldn't be a problem," said the fourth man, a short fellow with thinning black hair. He put his hand on my shoulder and pulled himself closer. "I hear Mango's an old crop-duster pilot. I been told he's been known to dust a field right in front of a Class Five tornado." He seemed to think that was uproariously funny.

He obviously didn't care who heard him.

"Where did you hear that?" Mango said, frowning.

"From most of the crew out there in the hanger," the man laughed.

"Only did that one time," Mango said, frowning again as he picked up his pace.

"Once is enough, ain't it?" the man said, still laughing.

"I'm only going tonight if it's all clear," Mango said, "No matter what those fools in the hanger say."

He was muttering *"Damn tourists"* to himself as he opened the door to the little plane. I don't think he realized I heard him but, looking at him, I decided even if he did, he probably didn't care. I could tell by his swagger.

"Nobody else has luggage?" Mango asked, without a trace of surprise in his voice. Other than the big shooter with the valise, I was the only one with a carry-on bag.

"I'm going overnight," I said, embarrassed.

"Don't worry about it," Mango said, as his smile returned. "I get lotsa folks who only bring wallets and checkbooks on this hop." His glance at the other two was obvious. "I'll put your case behind the last seat."

As Mango opened the rear-opening second door to the Cessna, the wind began to howl and the windsock atop the hanger started a furious flapping. So furious, I thought it might blow right off the pole.

"See what I mean about the wind?" the beefy baccarat player said again. "You sure it's okay to fly?"

Mango ignored him.

"You two sit here in the back," he said, pointing at the beefy guy and the balding passenger. "I'll let Red sit up front, with me." He winked at me. "Two red-heads add some balance, don't ya think?"

I liked Mango, and couldn't help smiling. Besides, the two seats in the rear were cramped, at best. "I guess so," I said. "At least they'll see us coming."

"With that scar on your puss, *Mater*, they won't soon forget us, either," Mango said. He seemed to study me carefully when I remained silent.

"Touchy subject?" Mango added, after a few moments.

"Vietnam," I told him.

"'Nuff said." he grunted. "Marine?"

"Navy," I said.

His eyebrows both shot up.

"I didn't think Navy guys saw all that much action over there," he said.

"It's a long story," I whispered.

"Yeah, and it's a short flight," *Beefy* said, interrupting. "At least it if we ever get our asses off the ground." Mango snorted at that, but started the engine.

"Close up them doors, ladies," Mango said, barking out his instructions, "unless you brought your own chute and you're planning on doing some parachute jumping when we get out over the Mojave."

I could feel the plane shaking from the wind as we taxied to the only runway servicing the field.

Apparently reporting what he was hearing in his headphone, Mango added, "You might have noticed the wind tonight, but the Tower says there's a brief letup between each gust." He moved the mouthpiece of his headset and looked around the plane. "If everybody's ready," he said, "we'll go during one of the next lulls."

"Is it really safe?" the beefy guy asked again, clutching his valise to his chest.

"This thing don't need much time on the runway," Mango answered, "I could probably take off with it from the top of a chest of drawers."

I couldn't help laughing again.

"That may be true," said the little balding guy, wiping heavy perspiration from his prodigious forehead as he looked at me, "but let's agree...no barnstorming tonight, okay Mango?"

"No more than it takes," Mango grinned as he leaned over and whispered to me, "Gotta tell those guys in the hanger to keep their damn mouths shut."

He touched the headset, appeared to be listening and said something on the radio in response to the tower. He turned his head in my direction and smiled again...and gunned the engine.

"Here we go," he said.

The little plane lurched forward and was just beginning to rise from the ground when the temperamental wind gusts picked up speed from their momentary lull. I could feel the Cessna rock from side to side, as it began to howl outside again. It was the fiercest the wind had blown all night.

There was another moment of blessed silence as the wind suddenly dropped when I could hear the roar of the engine again as the little Cessna struggled to climb.

Just as I began to think everything was going to be okay, the wind shrieked louder than ever and something seemed to slam into the plane. It felt like it had hit us just behind the prop and right under my seat. The whole plane shuddered.

Oh shit...this doesn't feel right.

"Dammit!" Mango shouted, and the tremor in his voice echoed the fear that had my heart hammering, as the plane's nose rose sharply and the left wing seemed to spin up to the clouds in the sky.

I don't remember hitting the ground, although I know we must have. I opened my eyes and the world was upside down. I was still strapped in, hanging in my seat, and the roof was only inches away from my face. I was having trouble focusing and realized something was in my eyes.

It was blood.

I put my hand up to wipe it away, and my forehead thundered when I touched it. *Shades of Sydney*, I thought, remembering the car crash in Australia while on leave from duty in Vietnam.

For some reason, the only thought running through my mind was, *I wonder what happened to my buddy, Evan Brisson? I haven't seen him since that damn accident on leave in Australia.*

It was going to be the last thought I had for a while.

CHAPTER 15 - Sticks

Funny how things happen. It was only pure luck I saw the damned old article at all. The Brickdale newspaper was already in the wastebasket, buried under the local New York dailies, when I first saw caught sight of the headline.

I had just returned from a month-long facilities tour with three new clients. I followed that miserable glad-handing grind with a much-appreciated two-week vacation to Acapulco, where I chased more than a few skirts, sampled more than my share of tequila and soaked up way too much sun, so the paper was really old by the time I actually saw it.

My first reaction, when I spied it in the debris, was to ask myself, for perhaps the ten-thousandth time, why I bothered to subscribe to that awful Brickdale rag at all. I seldom, if ever, read the damn thing.

The file cabinets were full of old clippings we often used for reference, and they had recently been purged. The garbage was full and headed for the incinerator in the morning. If the front page of that particular edition had been tossed into the wastebasket face down, the headline *Horrific Interruption to Local Wedding* would never have caught my eye in the first place.

The headline wasn't actually what originally grabbed my attention. It was the half-page picture that accompanied the article. Ordinarily, knowing the kind of pap that sometimes passes for news, I might have ignored that too, except there was a face in the picture I recognized.

Janice Patton, from Reichold Street.

She pouted out of that grainy black and white on the front page, looking every bit as beautiful as I remembered her, even with the shattered remains of what looked like a smoldering car in the background.

She was in a wedding dress, which was torn...both at the sleeve and in a big gash across her shoulder. Her hair was disheveled and her eye makeup was smeared all over her face, apparently from a long bout of crying. Hardly a fashion glamour shot.

Still, I thought she was gorgeous. When I saw her picture, I dug the paper out of the trash and after I read the whole article, I was stunned.

However, it wasn't the dreadful riot that seemed to have taken place during poor Janice's wedding reception that surprised me. The surprise came when I looked closely at her companion in the photo.

Sonofabitch.

That was my first thought when I read the caption.

She didn't marry Paul, was my second.

I think most of us living on Reichold Street in that old neighborhood would have given huge odds against Janice marrying anyone in our group but Paulie, but there it was in black and white.

Mr. and Mrs. Randy Camron.

I read it again, just to be sure. I had to dig in the trashcan to find the other pages and finish the article. Paulie was mentioned in the first paragraph of copy on the jump page. *Paul Barrett,* it said, *noted thriller novelist* had been one of the special guests in attendance, but he was not the groom. The listing also gave the names of several of his books, some published under a pen name.

Sonofabitch, I thought, for a second time.

That's our Paulie? A best-selling author?

"Hey, Maxie," I yelled across the tops of the cubicles to my production manager, "don't we do some sort of design work for a few of those big publishers?"

"Not much," she said, standing so I could see her tossing her long dark hair back over her shoulders. "Just a few posters and some trade ads for a couple of their lesser sci-fi authors."

"Like who?" I said.

"Beats the hell out of me," Maxie said, "but they're all aliens with tentacles, big-chested broads in tights and spaceships." She shook her head and pouted. "You should know, you designed most of them."

I didn't like the snickering I heard coming from several cubicles, but I let it go. I thought Maxie was cute when she pouted like that. It was the main reason I'd hired her. She wasn't really all that good as a graphic designer, but she was lots of fun to look at. She reminded me a whole lot of Janice Patton.

"Did you know I grew up on the same street with one of the big-time publishing names?"

"Yeah, sure you did," she snickered, "just like I used to date Albino Luciani...you know, before he became Pope."

"John Paul the First," I said as I walked over to her cubicle, "that's probably what killed him so fast, dating a broad like you." I thought she'd be impressed I knew the Pope's real name, but she didn't take my joke very well.

She gave me another one of her insolent, sexy little pouts and then crossed herself before she turned her back on me completely to let me know I had pissed her off.

"I just said that. I didn't really *date* him," she said. "You shouldn't say things like that."

The snickering in the cubicles grew even louder.

"No...really," I said, calling after her, wishing I could learn to think a little before I opened my mouth. "Paul Barrett...the novelist...grew up on the same street I did."

"Who?"

"Paul Barrett," I said.

"Sure he did," Maxie scoffed.

"No, really," I said, not wanting her to walk away. I handed her the old news article. "This is him, right here."

She took the paper, but didn't stop walking.

"In fact," I added, "Paulie was one of my best friends. He's the one who gave me my nickname."

She stopped and turned, with a little smirk on her face. "Oh, is he the one who named you *Sticks?*"

For a moment, it felt like I had been slapped.

"Yeah, Paulie was the very first one to call me that," I said, trying not to let her know how much it bothered me that she knew what the nickname was. I had been going to lie and tell her something else entirely. Something much more machismo and sexy.

"Paulie?" she said.

"That's what we all called him," I said. "Everybody I knew called him that."

"*Paulie* and *Sticks*. Sounds like there were a lot of nicknames flying around in your old neighborhood."

Maxie now had a *big* smirk on her face.

I wondered how many others in the office knew. As I glanced around at the cubicle walls and thought about what Maxie said, I realized it was probably everyone in the place.

"Yeah, I guess there were," I said, raising my voice as I smiled my best smile at her, "among other things. Would you like to know what *your* nickname would have been on Reichold Street?"

"If you were the one handing them out," she said, "I can guess. You never look any higher than my chest."

"That's not true."

"No?" she said. "Then what color are my eyes? You've known me for almost a year and a half. You should have seen them at least once."

"They're green," I said.

"Lucky guess," she said. She walked up and poked me in the arm.

"Yes, it was," I smiled. I didn't tell her I'd noticed at her first interview because she looked so much like Janice, except Janice's eyes were an azure blue.

I gave her backside a playful slap. Maxie jumped and tried to look indignant. I ignored her. I glanced at the article again to refresh myself about Paulie's general location. Then I called Bobby, the office gopher. I knew he was listening to our conversation, just like everyone else.

"Hey, Bob-o," I said when he arrived, "go look up some info for me on the novelist in this article...Paul Barrett...and while you're at it, see if he has an address listed anywhere near San Diego."

There was more snickering behind the cubicles, and when Bobby didn't move right away, I waved my arms in his face. "C'mon," I said, trying to make myself sound angry. "*Chop-chop.* Now. Get move on. Or should I look for your replacement? If I needed that bio sometime tomorrow I would have asked you tomorrow." Bobby got a panicked look on his face and ran off.

The people in each cubicle kept their heads down the rest of the afternoon.

Bobby got back to me just a few minutes before quitting time, with the information I had asked for, along with a page torn out of a more recent Brickdale paper.

"What the hell is that?" I said, pointing at the torn paper.

"Thought you might like to see it," he said. He was panting. "You're originally from Brickdale, aren't you?"

"What of it?" I half expected the article to be about something less than socially acceptable. *What else would they print in that rag?*

I was also expecting some snide comment.

"A small plane crashed out in California late last night" Bobby said, "with a writer from Brickdale on it."

"No shit," I said.

I snatched the torn paper from his hand and there it was: *Local Author Randy Camron Seriously Injured in California Plane Crash.*

When I looked up, Bobby was still standing there.

"If you're waiting for a thank you," I said, "consider it done." When he still didn't move, I added, "Get the hell back to work...now."

I took a look at the info and walked over to Maxie's cubicle. I looked over the top of the cubicle wall, but didn't say anything right away. I was enjoying the view too much.

I finally asked her, "Want to take a trip?"

"Not really," she said. Her tone of voice let me know she had seen me leering over the wall the whole time. When she looked up she added, "Where to?"

I looked again at the bio on Paul Barrett and compared it to the hospital they said Randy was taken to after the crash. *Scripps Memorial in La Jolla.* "West coast," I said. "Sunny southern Cal."

"I don't know..." she started to say.

While she hesitated, I added, "San Diego. Corporate expense account."

I could tell by the way she turned around in her chair she was interested. I figured she was like a lot of girls... enamored of my fancy car and my wallet. I had known when I hired her that my bankroll was a much bigger draw than I was. Always has been.

Besides, Maxie was rumored to like to party. It had been the main reason I hired her. She wasn't that good a designer. I figured she'd jump at the chance to travel...even with me. The corporate expense account meant we'd be staying in five-star hotels and eating at fancy restaurants.

"Okay," she said, "where we goin'?"

"Call LaGuardia and book us a couple of seats to San Diego," I said to her, adding, "First class, of course. And get us a car. A *nice* one. Oh...and book the best suite at the Grande Colonial in La Jolla. At least two nights. No...better make it three." She giggled when I said, "We'll see what happens from there."

"Something special going on?"

"Don't know yet," I said, "but never leave opportunity knocking...it's bad luck."

"When do you want the tickets?"

"You doing anything tomorrow?" I asked.

"I am now," she said.

CHAPTER 16 - Philly

I saw the article in a tabloid that was laying on the counter while I was standing in line at Carl's Beer & Wine to pay for my six-pack. I bought some of those sleazy tabloids once in a while, because the old lady liked to read the shit about movie stars, even if it wasn't true.

Most of it was the same phony bullshit they always printed in those rags, *Aliens Land in Washington, D.C.* and *Four-headed Baby Born Speaking Three Languages.*

I picked this one up because of the little inset picture in the corner of the lead article. It was a mug shot of *Micah,* my one-time boss. He was also the sonofabitch who cut my thumb when he was looking for his money when he first got out of the slammer.

I rubbed the scar on my thumb as I read. Damned spot still hurt once in a while, even though it was long healed.

The article talked about Micah's attack on the Camron wedding reception. I knew all about that, of course, because it was old news, but I was hoping it would also say what had happened to Micah. I knew he'd been arrested after that wedding fiasco and I guessed he'd been sent back to the big house, but no one, inside or out, seemed to know anything about him.

At least, no one who was doing any talking.

That was unusual, to say the least.

Micah was not one to let grass grow under him, if you know what I mean. If he was back in the pen, he was gonna be running some operation, just like before, unless some other con stuck a shiv in him when he arrived.

We all knew that could easily happen...it does all the time...but I thought we woulda heard something by now. Cons, for all their blather about rat-finks and stoolies, can't ever keep their mouths shut for long.

"You wanna read it, you gotta pay for it," said the fat lady at the register. She laid her beefy arm protectively over the top of the old tabloid.

"C'mon," I said, grabbing the old rag and shaking it in her face, "this is an old issue you had on the table. Look at it. It's a goddam year or two old."

She started to object, until I opened my jacket and lifted my belly to let her see the Smith & Wesson I'd tucked into my jeans. I always carried it. Made me feel important. The old biddy had no way to know it wasn't loaded, but I had to laugh, because she shut up her lip and moved her fat arm in such a hurry.

"Tell ya what," I said, as I picked up the old tabloid, talking mostly to keep her away from the alarm button under the counter, "I'll actually buy one of them new ones for my old lady...but this old article I'm gonna read right here for free."

She didn't object, beyond a few mumbled curses, but reading it didn't tell me anything I didn't already know.

Way back when, I'd put out feelers all over town and still had no idea what happened to Micah. I'd even called my cousin in Chicago to see if someone over there had seen him, but no dice. He said he hadn't heard, but not to worry...maybe Micah was laying low or something, even if he was in the slammer again. Micah was probably avoiding the heat his notoriety would bring.

It sounded plausible to me.

I didn't hear anything to the contrary, so I still kinda expected to finally get some kinda notice from Micah about laundering money for him again in the state pen.

However, months and months went by with nothing.

I got antsy waiting. I kinda missed the ten percent I'd been getting, so one afternoon I drove over to the *Hot Cue* on Cherry Street to talk to Little Tony, who had been one of Micah's seconds, to see if he knew anything.

"He ain't comin' back," Tony said, but not before he checked me over to see if I was wearing a wire. A real paranoid, he was always thorough like that. "Thought you knew that."

"How was I supposed to know?"

"Most folks heard a long time ago."

I figured he was another asshole jiving around with me cause I'm slow sometimes. "What? He got life?"

"Worse than that," Tony snickered, "He got dead."

"Seriously? How?"

"You wouldn't believe it," Tony said, serious again.

"Try me."

He looked around as if checking to see if anyone else was paying any attention. I thought he was being funny, because there wasn't anyone else in the place.

"Some minor perp snuffed him."

"Snuffed Micah?" I couldn't believe anyone got the best of the man...he was *that* scary. "How?"

"Same day he got nabbed at that wedding screw-up," Tony said. "Some asshole in the jail infirmary wasted him with a pillow."

"A pillow," I said, almost laughing.

"Smothered him while he was shackled to a gurney."

"That was a while ago," I said, serious again.

Little Tony rolled his eyes, but just nodded.

"Sonofabitch," I said. "So, who's been calling the shots all this time?"

Tony got the funniest look on his face. "I been getting things passed to me," he said, "from Joe Candleman."

"From the hookah place? The water pipe store?"

"One and the same."

"Seems like an awful little fish to be runnin' things," I said. I thought someone bigger than old Joe would have stepped into the top local spot.

"Well, I hear he takes his orders from some dude in Chicago, but I ain't about to ask him...are you?" Tony said. "You ready to question who's in charge?" The way Tony looked at me made my skin crawl.

I knew asking a lot of questions was an easy way to wind up in a cheap pine box, or worse...being buried without any box at all by the side of some lonely dirt road.

The thought scared the shit out of me.

"I just wondered, is all," I said.

"Why? You wanna talk to him or what?"

"Hell, no," I said.

Little Tony smiled and gave me a dismissive little sniff.

"I'm just glad there was no way they could blame that whole *Micah* fiasco on me," I said. "Sonofabitch musta cost 'em a ton."

"You ain't got nothin' to worry about," Tony said. He turned his back on me. "We all knew *you* weren't gonna be the one calling the shots."

"How?" I smiled back. "Is that what Micah told you? Could be a cover story, ya know."

"Not likely," Tony said, turning around, "Everybody from here to Toledo knows you're fifty cents shy of a dollar."

"That ain't always true," I said.

I showed him the old Brickdale paper I'd picked up at Carl's party store, and he laughed at me. "We all know what happened out there, Philly. Most of us on this side of town were part of it, remember?"

"Well," I said, "sometimes I'm ahead of the curve."

"What the fuck does that mean?"

"It means, smart guy, you've probably not seen *this* yet." With my right hand, I held up the Brickdale paper from last month. *Two Local Authors on Extended Book Tour* was the headline.

"What the hell is that to me?" Tony snorted.

"These are the guys Micah wanted...the ones you say got him killed. They were gonna wind up this tour thing in San Diego." I shook the paper for emphasis.

"So what?" Little Tony said. The way he backed-up a step told me I'd surprised him.

"You got people on the coast, don't you? These two musta cost you nearly seven figures, not to mention taking out one of your top guys," I said.

"Again," Tony said, stepping back, "so what?"

"I'm a little surprised, is all. How do you guys keep control around here?"

"You better be watchin' your mouth, Philly," Tony said, "you're walkin' on dangerous ground."

"Not from where I sit," I said. I couldn't keep the smirk off my face. I seldom felt like I had the upper hand like I did now. "I bet most of the boys have the same question runnin' through their heads that I do."

"Oh yeah? What question?" Tony said, taking the bait.

With my left hand, I held up the latest Brickdale rag with the headline *Local Author Randy Camron Seriously Injured in California Plane Crash.*

"When did you guys stop getting revenge?"

I let my words sink in. Little Tony's right eyebrow shot up, so I knew I had his attention.

CHAPTER 17 - Janice

The phone rang the first time at a quarter to seven in the morning. I was already up but I was in the shower, so I missed it. It rang again a few minutes later and I missed that one, too. It rang a third time right after I finished rinsing the shampoo out of my hair.

Persistent, I thought, *at this hour it must be Randy.*

I wondered why he was calling so early. It wasn't even four o'clock on the coast.

The phone was still ringing when I stepped out of the tub, wrapped a towel around myself and ran to answer it.

"Hello?" I said, trying to think of something sexy to say to Randy. It's a good thing I didn't, because it wasn't my sweet husband on the phone at all.

"Mrs. Camron? Mrs. Randall Camron?"

I didn't recognize the voice. "Yes, who is this?"

"This is Sergeant Ryan Pierson, Mrs. Camron, with the Brickdale Police Department."

"Police?" I said, "Is something wrong?"

"Yes, ma'am. If you don't mind I need to talk to you about your husband."

To have someone supposedly from Brickdale on the line, I thought Randy had put someone up to making a prank call. I fully expected to hear him laughing in the background at any moment.

"Oh dear," I said, going along with the joke. "Does he need to be bailed out again? What's he done this time?"

"I wish that's all it was, Mrs. Camron," the voice on the phone said, "but I'm afraid I have some bad news."

I've had lots of bad news in my life. I'll never be one to think the phrase *'my heart was in my throat'* is a bunch of hokum over it, because I've experienced it more times than I care to count. I know it's true. The way the officer said *bad news* he sounded so serious I knew this wasn't some kind of joke. Not even Randy would stoop that low.

I don't remember thinking anything else at all, but I'm sure my heart may have stopped beating for a moment. I couldn't inhale. I couldn't talk.

"Are you still there, ma'am?" the sergeant said.

"Yes." I could barely whisper the word.

"We had a phone early call this morning from the police department out in La Jolla, California..." Sergeant Pierson seemed to hesitate, as if he was searching for the right words to say. "There was a plane crash very late last night at a small airport near there."

I could feel the air rush out of my lungs.

"They normally let the hospital call the next of kin," Sergeant Pierson continued, "but one of the officers out there had apparently attended some sort of book event your husband was involved in, and he was one of the first responders."

Next of kin? Omigod.

"He asked us to call, so you wouldn't have to wait for the hospital to get around to it. He knows they sometimes drop the ball."

There was a long silence on the phone as those words kept running through my mind...*hospital...next of kin.*

As they did, my knees started to shake. I dropped the towel and sat down, stark naked and still dripping wet, on the edge of the bed. I dropped the phone, too, and it took me several fumbling moments to pick it up again.

"Hello...hello..." Sergeant Pierson was saying.

"Yes, I'm here," I whispered.

"Ma'am, there's no easy way to say this," the sergeant sighed, "but I'm afraid your husband was on the plane that crashed early this morning."

I just sat there and stared at the receiver, like that piece of black plastic was something evil and alive.

"Mrs. Camron?" Sergeant Pierson said. "Are you still there? Are you all right?"

After moments of barely being able to whisper, I found myself almost screaming. "What happened? Is he alive? Please tell me he's alive. How bad is he hurt?"

My hands trembled so much I almost dropped the damned telephone again.

Omigod, Omigod. My heart started to hammer.

"Mrs. Camron," the sergeant said, "please calm down. As far as I know, your husband is still alive. But they tell me he's in critical condition. He's been transported to the Scripps Memorial Hospital in La Jolla." He relayed all the information he had, repeating it twice. He had to repeat it a third time before I finally wrote it all down.

As he did, I remembered the sound of the Sheriff pounding on the front door years ago when my mother had her accident, and my voice sounded more like the whimper of a little girl than the grown woman I'm supposed to be.

"What am I supposed to do?" I said, when I could breathe again.

"I'd suggest you arrange a flight to California as soon as you can," the Sheriff said. "It sounds like your husband might need you." It was such a simple statement, but in my heart I knew what he was really saying was something far more sinister.

It might be the last time you ever see him.

I called Donnie right away. He was as shocked as I had been, but he kept his composure on the phone with me, which I thought was a surprise.

"I'll call the airport about tickets and get us a cab," he said, taking charge, "Then I'll be right over to pick you up." He seemed powerful and authoritative, a lot like he was before all his trouble began.

The whole time he talked, I kept thinking, *Isn't it nice, the old Donnie is back*? I don't know why. I guess I'd gotten used to the way he stumbled through conversations after he was shot.

It gave me an odd feeling, to be at once happy for him and yet scared to death about my husband.

As I waited for Donnie to arrive with the cab, I paced the floor. I saw Jimmy Lewis' letter sitting on the table and felt hot anger wash over me. Crying, I tore it into dozens of little pieces and threw it away. There was no way on earth I'd ever bother Randy with it, assuming I got the chance.

Assuming. Dear God.

I kept telling myself *this can't be happening*...although I knew damned well it could.

CHAPTER 18 - Paul

It took me a few moments to shake the sleep out of my eyes when the telephone rang. I was dreaming about Carrie and the old condo we lived in when we first got together. The dream seemed so real I was reaching in the wrong direction to shut off my clock alarm before I realized it was the phone.

It was a struggle to bring things into focus, so the phone was on its fourth or fifth ring before I finally picked it up. My throat was so dry and tight, my voice was hoarse and barely recognizable, even to myself. I thought I must sound half-drunk to whomever was calling.

"Hello," I mumbled.

The clock on the nightstand said it was four-fifteen. The sun wasn't up yet, and it was far earlier than I was used to getting out of bed.

"Paul? Paul Barrett? Is that you?"

"This is Paul Barrett," I said, yawning. I was still half asleep. "Who the hell is this?" It was hard for me to be civil when awakened at that hour of the morning.

"Paulie," the voice said again, just this side of sounding familiar, "it's me, Don Camron."

I'm not sure whether it was his name that clicked first, or his use of the diminutive everyone from Reichold Street had used to address me for all those years...*Paulie*...but I was suddenly wide-awake.

"Donnie?" I said. "Donnie? Is that really you?"

"It's really me, Paulie," he said, "and...oh shit, I'm so sorry...I'm in Brickdale, and I just realized what time it must be out there..." His voice kind of drifted to a halt, as if he was embarrassed to have called so early.

"It's all right, Donnie," I said, "what's going on?"

"Paulie, I need your help."

"Anything, my friend, you know that."

"It's my b-brother," I could hear the edge in his voice and realized he sounded close to tears.

"Randy?" I said, apprehensive. "What's going on?"

"There's been a plane crash," Donnie said.

"Omigod, no." I could feel icy fingers around my heart. "Is he all right?"

"No, he's not," Donnie's voice quavered again like he was going to cry. "We were on a book tour, Paulie. The first goddam one we ever got to do together..."

"What happened?" I said, "Where is he?"

"He's in the hospital...and I'm on my way out there again to be with him. He was with me in La Jolla yesterday morning for the last stop on our tour."

"La Jolla? You were out here?"

"Yeah," Donnie said, "and we were having such a great time." His sigh seemed to shake the phone. "We were going to look you up after the signing, Paulie, but Roger Craig said you were probably busy."

There was another long silence.

"You're not in La Jolla, are you?" I was confused.

"No," Donnie said, "I told you, I'm in Brickdale. We were both going to go back home together, and then Randy changed his plans. He wasn't going directly back home at all. He was going to fly to Vegas first, just for the hell of it."

"You didn't go with him?"

"He wanted me to," Donnie said. "He even cleared it with Janice. She tried to talk me into it, too, when we called her."

"So why didn't you go?"

As I said the words I realized I wouldn't be having this conversation at all, if he had. He'd have been on the same plane with his brother.

"I was tired, Paulie. I was worn out," Donnie said. "All I wanted was to go home. When we told her, Janice said she would pick me up at the airport, so I left him there and caught the last plane back east."

There was another long moment of silence I couldn't fill. Even though I make up dialogue for a living, I couldn't find the words. Just when I thought I should interject something, *anything*, Donnie spoke again.

"Randy told me to go ahead and go home," Donnie volunteered in my silence. "He usually went everywhere with me, but he thought I could finally handle traveling on my own again. I was sure I could, too, but I didn't want him to go to Las Vegas alone. I had a bad feeling about it."

"Oh, Donnie..."

There was another silence. From the sound of it, Donnie was trying to catch his breath.

"I thought about calling you last night," he said, "to have you talk to him...but it was already late there, and I figured I shouldn't surprise you like that."

I still couldn't find any words to say. I cradled my forehead with my free hand and thought about the phone call I hadn't made.

"He booked a small, private plane to take him to Vegas early this morning, our time," Donnie said. "Cheapest one he could find, knowing him. He figured he only had a day, and he wanted to get there early so he would have time to take it all in."

"He isn't...dead, is he?" I dreaded the answer.

"No, Paulie," Donnie said, with a noticeable tremor in his voice, "at least he wasn't when they called Janice this morning. Two other passengers were killed. They said his plane flipped over on takeoff. They took Randy and the pilot to Scripps Memorial Hospital in La Jolla." He stopped and it sounded like he was trying to catch his breath.

"How is Janice taking it?"

"She called me right after she heard," Donnie said. "She couldn't stop crying."

"I can imagine," I said. Then his comments caught up to my sleep-addled brain. "Did you say he's at Scripps in La Jolla? That's practically in my back yard."

"I know," Donnie said, "that's why I called you. I don't know much more about it yet. They told her his condition is critical, and when I called them they said we should get there right away, but..."

He hesitated, and I heard a small sob.

"Go ahead, Donnie," I said, "it's all right."

"It looks like it will be sometime late tonight before Janice and I can possibly get out there..." he hesitated for another moment, and I knew what was coming next. "I don't want him to be alone, Paulie."

"I'm on my way," I told him.

"Could you?" he said, the relief evident in his voice, "you don't mind? I mean, we don't know anyone else out there, except Roger...but..."

"Donnie," I said, "of course I'll go. I won't let him be alone. I promise. *No man left behind.* You can meet me when you get to the hospital. You and Randy have always been like brothers to me...you know that."

There was a long silence on his end.

"Besides," I said, "I owe each of you more than I can ever repay in this lifetime."

"You don't owe us a thing," Donnie said, "but bless you...bless you." He said it several more times, crying now without trying to hide it.

"Is Janice with you now?" I said. I wanted to tell her personally I would stay beside Randy.

"I'm on my way to get her," Donnie said, "I'm just waiting for the cab I called to get here." He paused a moment, then started to sob again.

"Donnie, are you all right?" I asked, already knowing what his answer would be.

"I'm scared," he said.

"Listen, Donnie," I said, "Just deal with it as it comes. When you get your flight information, call me. If I'm not home, it's because I'm already on my way to the hospital to see your brother, so leave a message. Okay?"

"Okay..." Donnie sniffed.

"You remember my housekeeper, right? Jasmine?" I could imagine him nodding, but Donnie was silent, so I kept going. "I'll leave a note," I said, "She gets here at nine, and she'll know how to get hold of me. I'll also arrange for someone to pick you up at the airport. It will probably be Roger, but if not him *someone* will be there, I promise."

"Thanks, Paulie." His voice sounded for a moment like it had when we were kids. I could hear his huge sigh.

"Look for Roger or some guy holding a sign with your name on it," I said, "I'll get over to Randy. You just take care of Janice, and get to the hospital as fast as you can."

"I will." I could hear a rustling. "The cab is here."

"Good. Get going."

As soon as Donnie hung up, I got dressed, made myself a cup of coffee and downed a quick bowl of cereal. It was a purely instinctual reaction, because I realized I didn't know when I'd have a chance to eat again.

The sun was coming up, so I walked around the house, switching off all the lights, wondering if a phone call to Brickdale when I first thought of doing it the evening before, would somehow have let me keep Randy off that plane.

Woulda-coulda-shoulda was the sad mantra that ran through my mind. I knew I'd said that same damn thing many times before, and just like before, I knew there was nothing I could do about it now.

CHAPTER 19

I was headed out the door when Donnie called back. "I'm glad I caught you," he said. "I wanted to tell you we've got stand-by seats on a flight scheduled into San Diego this afternoon...a little after four o'clock. All we have to do is get to the airport at this end in time. We're about to get into the cab to Capitol City Airport. It'll be close, but they said they'll hold the tickets until the plane starts to board."

"I'm going through the door right now," I said, as I wrote down his flight information, "I'm on my way to the hospital. Should be there in thirty minutes."

"Bless you," he said, and I couldn't help hearing the tense edge that had crept into his voice again.

"Take it easy, Donnie," I said, trying to reassure him, "and don't worry about this end of things. I'll stay with

Randy until you get here, and I'll have someone pick you up at the airport."

"Roger Craig?"

"I haven't called Roger yet, but if it isn't him *someone* will be there, I promise. Look for someone with your name on a sign. I'm heading over to be with your brother." I was doing my best to calm him down,

"Thanks, Paulie," Donnie said.

"You two have a safe flight," I added, but I think Donnie had already hung up.

As soon as I got off the phone with Donnie, I called Roger Craig. I asked him to get our friends at the airport. They all knew each other, so it would be easy to find one another. He hemmed and hawed about it for a moment, like he had something else to do that he didn't really want to discuss, but as soon as I told him what was going on he was on board.

"Shit," he said, "a plane crash?"

"Yeah...Donnie said a couple of passengers died."

Roger was suddenly full of questions. He rattled them off without seeming to pause for a breath.

"Is Randy all right? Did you know I just saw him and his brother yesterday morning? I dropped him off at his book signing in La Jolla, but he told me he didn't need to be picked up...said he'd already made plans. He talked about calling you. Did he? I thought maybe he'd gotten hold of you. What did he say? Did you know about his plans last night?" He prattled on for several more moments, without seeming to pause for a breath.

I told him what I knew about Randy changing his plans to fly to Vegas. I could hear Roger tap impatiently on the receiver like he always did when he was nervous.

"You okay, *Dodger*?"

"Why didn't he say something?"

"You all right?" I asked again.

"No, I'm not," Roger said. "Why didn't they tell me? I figured they were coming out to see you. I even told them they should. Why would Randy go to Las Vegas alone?" The tapping on the phone got more insistent. "Damn it, he never listens to me any better than you do."

There was another long pause in our conversation when we both seemed at a loss for words.

"He never showed up here...never even called," I said. "Donnie told me this morning Randy thought I'd be too busy to just drop in like that, so he apparently decided to go to Vegas by himself alone before he went back."

I could hear Roger take a deep breath. "Oh Christ," he said, "I'm the one who told him you'd probably be too busy for him just to drop in. All I meant was he should call you first. What the hell happened?"

"I don't know the particulars," I told him. "Donnie said it was a small plane that flipped over on takeoff. Randy's condition is critical, but that's as much as I know. Donnie and Janice are on their way out here."

"You want me to get them?"

He was becoming adept at anticipating my questions. "Yeah, Roger, I do," I sighed. "I need you to pick them up at the airport and get them to the hospital. I've got to get my ass over there with Randy now. I promised. I owe it to both of them."

Roger took their flight information and the address of the hotel, and I could hear another deep sigh. This seemed to be the day for them. "You be careful driving," he said, "We don't need to have anything happen to you, too...and, damn it, let me know what's going on."

"I will, Roger. I will."

"Don't worry about your friends. I'll take care of things on this end when they get here."

I think I thanked him, but I really don't remember.

Scripps Memorial Hospital is normally less than thirty minutes away from my house, but traffic was heavy that morning and it seemed to take an eternity to get there.

It didn't help my psyche at all that Scripps Memorial was the same hospital the ambulance had transported us to after the accident all those years ago. I remembered all too clearly the small trickle of blood that started from the corner of Carrie's mouth right after the crash, looking like a small red teardrop, oddly out of place on her lip.

"I'm scared, Paul. Hold me."

When the ambulance arrived for Carrie that night, I also vividly remembered watching them as they moved her into it, while I was still trapped in our car. I remember her limp arm dangling over the side of the stretcher, swaying slightly with the movement of the EMT's. It was a memory that invaded my dreams almost nightly for a long time.

It still creeps up on me once in a while, even now. When I wake from that dream, I have to try to force my mind back to pleasant things, but it's a useless exercise.

I remember reading Voltaire in college. *To believe in God is impossible; not to believe in Him is absurd.*

I guess I really don't know one way or the other. I've never been strongly religious, but I prayed very hard for my Carrie on the way to the hospital that night. *Worthless waste of time*, is what I thought now of my effort.

Still, I prayed all over again on my way to see Randy, hoping the whole time I would find him alive...not knowing what I was going to do if he wasn't.

Tell me this isn't happening.

Seeing the hospital building looming ahead of me put an immediate end to my prayers. My whole body started to tremble when I got close enough to see the complex again. It got so bad I had to pull over to the shoulder and stop, shut off the engine and close my eyes until it passed.

Scripps was where I had to identify Carrie's body after they officially pronounced her dead that awful night, and I have no pleasant thoughts at all about that place.

I wondered again if there was anyone at all in Heaven to hear my pleadings, because I wasn't sure I could bear having to go in and identify Randy, too. For a moment, I allowed myself to think I had been cursed, since awful things seemed to follow my life and the lives of so many of my friends. With an effort, I forced all those thoughts out of my mind, took a deep breath and restarted the car.

The morning sun flashed off the two-story glass façade of the building as I slowly drove into the emergency lot. My heart was pounding so hard my hands shook as I let go of the steering wheel, got out of the car and sprinted under the huge cement portico of the emergency entrance.

Please be alive, I said to myself, over and over.

I paused only a moment before I entered, to glance back and assure myself I had shut off the engine in the damned car...and to fervently wish I could be anywhere else on the planet but here.

CHAPTER 20

It took me a few moments to get my bearings when I stepped inside the massive lobby. I stopped at the information desk and waited for the woman to notice me. She had one hand over her eyes and spoke quietly into the headphone that clipped to her overdone white curls, obviously caught up in a private conversation. When I finally had her attention, I mentioned Randy's name.

"Randy Camron?" she said, putting her hand over the microphone while she looked at her register. "Are you a family member?" When I shook my head, she said, "I'm sorry sir, but Mister Camron is in intensive care. Only relatives are allowed in."

"His brother wanted me to be with his brother until family could get here. He should have notified someone. My name is Paul Barrett."

"Look," she said softly to whomever was on the phone, "I have to go. Someone's here. I'll call you back."

She seemed a little flustered as she searched her log. "Let me check, Mister Barrett," she said. She kept glancing up at me, frowning.

"Is there a problem?"

"No," she said, "It's just...I *thought* I recognized you when you came in."

"I get that a lot," I said.

"You look awfully familiar."

I smiled, trying to be as charming as I could, while wishing this whole procedure was over. "I guess I've got one of those *everyman* faces."

"On the contrary, Mister Barrett, you have a very nice face," The color rose in her cheeks as she blushed, "and I'm almost certain I've seen you before."

"Well...I *was* here as a patient a few years ago..." I couldn't bring myself to mention Carrie.

"No, that isn't it," she said, "I almost never remember the patients...just their visitors."

I checked her name on her receptionist's badge and sighed. "Let me ask you something, Madge," I said, "do you read a lot?"

"All the time, but what does that..." she started to say, but she stopped and looked up at me. "That's it!" Her voice was excited but the words were a whisper. "Your face. I've seen you on the back cover of your books."

111

"Bingo," I said, shutting my eyes.

Her brow knitted in confusion. "But I don't remember anyone named Barrett on the family list."

"His brother said he'd take care of it," I said.

Madge frowned a little more, "Mister Camron didn't mention your name...oh, wait, yes, here you are..." she pointed at the monitor on the desk in front of her. "*Paul Barrett*. Right here," she poked at the screen, "plain as day. Don't know how I could have missed it. Mister Camron's brother did say you might be coming, and to let you in...because you're family."

"I'm glad you found me," I forced another smile. "Can I go up and see Randy now?"

"I didn't know there was a famous writer in their family," Madge said, ignoring my question.

"May I see him now?" I repeated.

I didn't pay any attention to two guys who got up from nearby seats during our conversation, until they stopped in front of me. One of them, dressed in levis and a plaid shirt, held an expensive-looking camera and flash. There was an ID badge for a local newspaper poking up out of the shirt pocket of the other one, with the edge of it stuck on his tie.

I don't really know what I expected at the hospital, but having to avoid newspaper reporters waiting in the lobby was never something that entered my mind.

"Did I hear you say you were here looking for Randy Camron," the one with the camera asked. "Would that be

Randy Camron, the writer?" His comment took me by surprise, although I don't know why it should have. I knew Roger had decided to work as their agent, and that Randy and Donnie had both recently published books.

I'd read some of Donnie's short stories years ago, when I tried to help him get started, and they were quite good. I suppose I'd just never thought of either one of them as an author. They were still *The Twins*, to me.

The reporters, pushing closer all the time, began to pepper me with questions. I got an immediate, first-hand exposure to the idea of violated personal space that was vastly different from the pressure of my fan base.

A few fans could be pushy. I didn't like it very much. These two were both pushy *and* obnoxious. I got forced away from the reception desk by their incessant pressure.

"Did you say he was a friend or a relative?" the one with the name badge asked. I saw him start a small tape recorder and point its tiny microphone in my direction. The next moment, it was right there in my face. "You and Mister Camron...where did you say you were going?"

I pushed his hand away.

"I don't remember saying anything...to either one of you." I made no attempt to hide my contempt for the two ambulance chasers. Ignoring my surliness, the asshole with the camera tried to pump me for still more information.

"Did you know where Mister Camron was going?" he said. "They said he had chartered a plane to Las Vegas.

113

Where was he going to stay in Vegas? Were you going with him? Did he gamble a lot? Were you meeting him there? Was he meeting someone else? When was he due back? Are you part of his family? Has the hospital told you anything about his current condition?"

He paused, focused his camera and the flash went off twice, right in my face. The light temporarily blinded me.

"Damn it, do you mind?"

I pushed him away again.

Madge, behind the information desk, motioned to me. The two obnoxious men stayed right behind me when I stepped back to the desk. I could hear them whispering to each other. She looked at the two reporters as she handed me a slip of paper with a few words written on it.

Room Number 733.

"Thank you," I said, as I took the note, thankful for the interruption...and the assistance.

"Don't mention it," she said. "I hope you don't mind if I tell you...I love your books." She looked embarrassed as she said it, more shy little girl than middle-aged woman.

"Thank you," I said again, "I'm glad you enjoy them." As I headed toward the elevators, I waved the little slip of paper at her. "Thank you for this, too. I owe you."

She grinned, which made her look a lot like the *Cheshire Cat* in *Alice in Wonderland*. "Enough to sign one for me?" She started to scrounge around on her desk and began scribbling on another little piece of paper.

I stepped back to her desk because I thought she had been writing her name. When I looked at the little piece of paper she held out to me, I saw it contained an address.

"I don't have a copy of one here," she said, "but perhaps you could send me a signed copy of your next one."

"Send you...?"

She cleared her throat and looked around the lobby before she answered. "I'm actually not supposed to let anyone but a *very close family member* go up to intensive care. Not *anyone*...if you get my drift."

"I understand," I said, waving her little note. "You'll get the very first edition."

Her grin dominated her lumpy face. I could barely see her eyes, it distorted her mouth and cheeks so much.

I was headed to the elevators twenty feet away, when she shouted. "Thank you, Mr. Barrett." Her voice seemed to reverberate in the otherwise quiet lobby.

The two reporters, who had stepped away from me, after deciding they weren't going to get any of the information they wanted, both looked up again in surprise when she shouted.

They turned almost as one and came back to me.

"Barrett?" the man with the camera said, squinting an eye at me. "Paul Barrett? The author? Are you Paul Barrett, the novelist?"

I ignored him and tried to move away, but he followed me to the elevator, never more than three steps behind. "Is Mister Camron an old friend of yours, Mister Barrett, or a business acquaintance?" the other one said, pushing his microphone at me again. "Were you going to meet him in Vegas? Are you two working together? Collaborating on something? Is that why you're here?"

"Look," I said, "who I am and why I am here is not any goddam business of yours...none. So, turn off that damned recorder and get that fucking camera out of my face."

"Did you get that," the fool with the microphone said.

"Every bit," said the asshole with the camera.

"You really are annoying," I muttered.

I pressed the little round elevator button repeatedly; more thankful than I can say when the little bell rang to announce its arrival. I almost started to breathe normally again. That is, until both reporters followed me into the car as I entered.

CHAPTER 21

I motioned to the receptionist. Madge had seen my little altercation with the reporters, because she had never taken her eyes off me. I hoped she would catch on when I gave her the 'phone' gesture with my hand, and nodded toward the security guard. If I could get her to call him, I'd let him deal with the reporters.

I had almost convinced myself it was going to be a futile effort, when my unspoken wish was granted. Madge was putting down her phone as the security guard, a beefy guy with close set dark eyes and a thick, muscular neck, stomped over from his cubicle.

It may have been my imagination, but he was so big the floor seemed to shake as he approached. "What's going on, here?" he said to the receptionist, in a voice about half an octave higher than his bulk predicted. "What's so urgent?"

As he waited for her to answer, he crossed his arms and looked sourly at me, as if I had to be the cause of all the commotion because I was blocking the elevator doors.

Without waiting for Madge to answer, I said, "I'd like these...gentlemen...to please step away from the elevator and quit following me."

"It's a free country," the one with the camera said. "We got as much right to use the elevator as this guy."

"Fine," I said, stepping out, "go ahead...use it."

Instead of going upstairs, the two reporters followed me out of the car.

"See what I mean?" I said, pointing at them.

"They the ones?" the guard asked Madge, also pointing at the reporters. She nodded and he turned to me. "Are they bothering you?"

"Yes, they are," I said. "Big time."

"Who are you going to see?" the guard asked.

"We're trying to see Randy Camron, the writer," the cameraman said, "He was brought here last night."

"And you," the guard said, looking at me.

"An old friend in ICU," I said. The two reporters both nodded, as if that was their answer, too.

"What floor are you going to?" the guard asked.

The two reporters just looked at each other.

"Seven," I said, which the fool with the camera echoed as soon as I spoke the word. I saw the receptionist shake her head. The guard saw her, too.

"I don't think so," he said. He put his hand on the shoulder of the guy with the camera and moved him back, away from me. With his free hand on the chest of the other one, he managed to push him back a step, too.

"You can't do this," the cameraman said. "It's a free country. We got rights."

They continued to protest, but the guard succeeded in pushing them both completely away from the elevator. I might have gotten away then, as the doors started to open back up again, but the guard stood in the doorway after I entered and that prevented them from closing.

As I stood in the back of the car, the photographer stepped forward and the flash on the camera went off one more time. The door started to close again and they kept pestering me with questions. "Mister Barrett, are you related to Mister Camron? How do you two know each other? Are you working together on a project? Why are you here? When will we be able to contact you again?"

"Barrett?" the guard said, "the writer?" The doors hit him and opened up yet again.

"Yes," I said. It came out as a sigh.

"Love your work," he said.

"Thank you," I said, "but honestly, can't you keep these two clowns away from me?"

"Yes, *sir*," the guard said.

As he nodded and stepped out of the doorway, he pushed the two men back another step.

119

"Wait a second," the cameraman said, doing his best to act indignant.

"Cool it, gentlemen" the guard said, "this is a hospital and I can't have you coming in here bothering the patients."

"He's not a patient," one of the reporters said.

"Would *you* like to be one?" I said, putting my hand on the open edge of door.

"What?"

"I'm sure you heard what I said." I was so pissed my voice was almost a hiss when the words came out. I stuck my finger in the face of the man nearest to me. "If you don't leave me alone, you're going to find yourself in here as a trauma patient...very, very soon."

I was more than a little angry now.

"Did you hear that?" The cameraman shouted to the guard. "That was a threat. That's assault."

He took a step forward, but the guard stopped him.

"Back off," the guard said.

The cameraman persisted. "This bozo just threatened us. Aren't you going to do something about it?"

"Seems to me it's the two of you," the guard said, gesturing at the two reporters, then crossing his massive arms, "who are causing all the commotion out here."

"Now see here," the second reporter chimed in, taking a step so he almost touched the giant guard's chest, "we got a right to be here same as him...you can't make us stop doing our jobs...you...you lousy *rent-a-cop*."

I could see the uniformed man bristle. He took a deep breath and expanded his already massive chest.

"If you two don't shut up," he said, "and quit annoying this man...I'm just liable to help him make it assault *and* battery." He looked over at Madge and winked. "You didn't hear that," he added.

She nodded at him. "Didn't hear a damn thing," she said, winking back.

She turned her head and winked at me, too.

"What the hell..." the cameraman started to say.

"Now...both of you," the burly guard said to the two reporters as he took a set of handcuffs from his belt, "I suggest you step away from this elevator...now."

Relieved, I watched him hold the two obnoxious men back with his arms as the door closed. "You haven't heard the end of this..." were the last words I heard. I couldn't tell which reporter they came from.

I took several deep breaths and listened to the sound of the machinery as the car rose, trying to calm myself before I got upstairs. It didn't seem to help very much. When the elevator reached the seventh floor, I stepped out into a silent hallway, directly across from another reception desk. I was thankful it hadn't stopped on any other floors on the way up.

There didn't seem to be any other visitors visible on the floor. I was delighted in that, too, because I didn't think I could repeat that whole charade in the lobby all over again, should the two somehow have managed to secure help on the upper floors.

Signs everywhere declared it was an ICU unit, and warned everyone to be quiet. The only person in sight was the nurse at the reception desk. I told her who I was, and who I was there to see. As she began looking up Randy's name, I asked her where Room 733 was located.

"Oh," she said, halting her search for a moment, "you must be the one Madge called about."

I wondered what Madge had told her, but when I didn't say anything, she resumed checking and finally nodded.

"Down the hall to your left, right at the corner and three units down on the left," she said, "and please be as quiet as possible." She looked up at me and added, "There are visitors in many of rooms, and a lot of the patients can't be exposed to any loud noises."

I was still so upset about the commotion downstairs, her directions to Randy's room didn't register. I felt like a fool, because I had to ask her to repeat them. She must have sensed my nervousness...or maybe she was afraid I'd do something stupid to disturb her patients. She sighed, got up and motioned for me to follow her down the hall.

As I made the slow walk with her down the ICU corridors to the room where they had my friend, I could hear monitors beeping in several of the curtained alcoves.

"Mister Camron is unconscious," she said, "so don't expect much from him in the way of communication."

I knew she was trying to prepare me for a rough time, and it reminded me of the evening I had walked down a similar corridor toward Carrie. That nurse hadn't said a word, even though she knew Carrie was already dead. I suppose giving that kind of news all the time wears on you so much it's easier sometimes not to say a thing.

That was when I realized why I had so much trouble concentrating on this nurse's comments. There was part of me that didn't want to know.

CHAPTER 22 - Puz

I was watching the local evening news, waiting for the football game that was scheduled to come on right after it finished, when a familiar face flashed across the TV screen. The moment I saw it, I yelled into the kitchen, trying to make myself heard over the blender.

"Tammy, come out here and look at this."

"I don't have time right now, Kenny..." she sighed.

"But you've gotta see this," I said.

"You know I don't care about the football game."

The tone of her voice carried all I had to know about her continued dislike of football. She blamed my limp on the game and seemed to forget entirely how it had kept me out of the service.

"It's not football...the game's not on yet," I said, watching a line of information scroll across the bottom of the screen. "Come and look, hon...you'll want to see this. It's Randy Camron."

"On the news?" I had to smile as she came into the room. She was almost running. "Is it about his book?"

I watched as the line of information disappeared and, once I read it, fervently wished I'd waited to find out why Randy's picture was on the tube before I said anything.

"No," I said, "I don't think so."

"Well," Tammy said, as she plopped down on the sofa, "it must be either about him or his brother. They've both been in the news a lot the last few weeks." She snuggled up close to me. "Isn't it neat so many of you guys from Brickdale have become famous?"

"We're hardly famous," I said.

"Well, Paulie certainly is," she said, "and Randy and Donnie have been on the news a lot lately." Tammy hugged my arm. "You were famous, too, for a little while."

"When was I ever famous?"

"When you were playing football...and then when you were making all those television commercials."

"That was a long time ago," I said, "Besides, I thought you were pissed because I played football."

"Silly," she said, snuggling closer, "You were always special...you know that. I just wish you hadn't gotten so messed up." She reached down to caress my gimpy knee, then looked over at the television. "If it isn't his book Randy's on TV about, what is it?"

"His plane crashed last night."

The television coverage had gone on to other things, but I watched my bride's eyes grow wide and her hands cover her mouth when I told her what had happened.

"Oh gosh, *Puz*," she said. "I'm so sorry." Tears formed in her eyes and she started to cry.

When she used the nickname for me all my friends had used, the one I knew she didn't like, I knew she was only humoring me...but it felt good to know that she cared.

"He was on a small charter flight going to Vegas."

"Are you sure?"

"It was just a quick announcement," I said. "I wouldn't have caught it at all, if they hadn't flashed his picture."

"You're certain it was our Randy?" Tammy said, a tiny glimmer of hope in her eyes.

"Positive," I said, "there's only one Randy Camron from Brickdale with that awful scar on his face."

She sniffled and snatched a Kleenex from the end table to wipe her nose. "How awful." She looked up at me and started to sob again. "After all your friend went through in his life...to die in a plane crash. There's no justice."

I held her as tears spilled down onto her cheeks.

After a moment, her sniffling stopped and a look of immense sorrow crossed her face. "Oh, poor Janice," she said, as she looked up at me.

I had been thinking about what the reporter was saying. "He isn't dead," I told her.

"What? But you said..." Tammy wrinkled her nose the way she always did when she was confused.

"He's not dead *yet*," I said. I reached over her for the telephone sitting on the table. "The news said he's in the hospital in critical condition...but that ain't dead."

"What are you doing?" Tammy asked.

"What a friend shoulda been doing all along," I said. "I'm calling Donnie Camron in Brickdale to see if he knows what's going on with his brother."

Tammy came to stand beside me, and the phone rang about fifteen times without an answer before I put it down.

"Well?" Tammy said.

All I could do was shrug at her. "There doesn't seem to be anyone home."

"They weren't *both* on the plane, were they?" Tammy had her hands over her mouth again, and her eyes were still glistening with tears.

"I really don't know," I said, wondering if I'd missed anything on the tube, "the news didn't say anything about Donnie...just his brother Randy."

I reached down and picked up the telephone again.

"Who are you calling now?"

"I'm going to try to get hold of Paulie," I said, "maybe he knows something."

"In California? Long distance?"

"Brickdale is a long-distance call from Tuscaloosa, too," I said. Tammy blushed when I looked at her.

"Of course," she said.

The phone at Paulie's house rang several times, and I thought I was going to strike out there, too. I was just about to hang up when someone answered it.

"*Buenos tardes,*" the voice said, "*la residencia del señor Barrett. Esta es Jasmine hablando.*"

"Hi, Jasmine," I said, recognizing Paulie's housekeeper. "This is Paul's friend, Ken Pozanski, calling. Is Paul there, by any chance?"

"*Hola, señor Puz,*" Jasmine said, using my nickname just like Paulie would. She sounded cheery. "*Señor Barrett no está aquí. Está en el hospital.*"

"The hospital...?" I started to say, before I realized he must be going to see Randy. "Oh, of course...Jasmine, is he going to see Randy Camron?"

"*Señor Camron,*" Jasmine said, after I said his name, "*Sí, se ha ido al hospital a ver al señor Camron. ¿Eres una de las personas que vienen a verlo, también?*"

I really didn't understand Spanish very well, but I knew just enough to know my assumption had been right. Paulie was at the hospital with Randy. What's more, it sounded like others were expected to be coming, too. She had to mean Donnie and Janice.

"Are Donnie and Janice there, too?" I asked.

"*Hermano del señor Camron y su mujer, sí.*"

I put my hand over the receiver. "His brother and his wife are out there," I said to Tammy.

"Thank goodness."

"Thank you, Jasmine."

I hung up without saying goodbye, before I thought about the abrupt disconnect sounding rude on her end.

"Well...?" Tammy said.

"Pack some clothes," I said, "it sounds like we're the only ones not there by Randy's side."

"We're going all the way to California?"

"He's got no family left," I said, "except for his wife and Donnie."

"Aren't they going to be out there for him?"

"I'm sure they are," I said, "Jasmine either said they were there, or they're coming." I could see the concern and doubt in her eyes. I hugged her for a second.

"Can we afford it?" she said. "Last minute tickets from here to San Diego are not going to be cheap."

"I can't afford *not* to go," I said. "They're going to need us, too. They're my *friends*, Tammy, my best friends."

I knew my answer was the right one in her book when she kissed my cheek.

"I love you, you big lug," she whispered.

"How fast can you pack?"

"Call the airport for the next flight and get us a cab," Tammy said, as she disappeared down the hallway, "I'll be ready by the time they get here."

I picked up the phone to dial Birmingham International Airport as I watched her head into our bedroom to pack a suitcase. Her sniffling had stopped and she marched deliberately ahead

God, I love that girl.

Then I thought about the way Janice was with Randy, and knew why Tammy had been crying.

CHAPTER 23 - Paul

Crossing the final sterile curtain in the doorway that separated Randy's cubicle from the rest of the ICU ward was the last thing I wanted to do. The nurse, whose name badge identified her as *Susan Bonner, RN*, had led me down the quiet hallways and entered Room 733 a moment before, but I hesitated.

When she'd gone in I'd caught a glimpse of Randy lying there, his red hair shaved completely off on one side, with electrodes attached to spots on his skull. There was an intravenous line in his right arm, a blood-pressure and heart rate cuff attached to the other.

The vital-signs monitor beeped softly as it kept vigil on his heartbeat. His pale body didn't move, except for the soft rise the ventilator brought to his chest. Without his personality active, the hideous scar on his face seemed even more pronounced. Once I saw him like that, I couldn't make my legs move to come any closer.

"Excuse me," the nurse said, poking her head back out of the curtain, "are you all right?"

"I...uh...yes, I'm fine," I stammered.

"It's okay," the nurse said, looking back at Randy, "I understand. It can be quite disconcerting at first. Take your time...as much as you need. I'll be right here."

Nurse Bonner stepped out and went a few steps down the hall. When she returned, she had a small chair with her.

"This is for you," she said, "the couple that *were* using it were moved down the hall a little while ago to the discussion room." She cleared her throat. "Family of a little girl...they'll be leaving tonight."

"Oh, is she getting out of ICU?"

"I guess you might say that," the nurse said. "They're unplugging the ventilator..." Blinking back tears, she looked away and didn't finish her statement. It was obvious the result wasn't going to be good.

"I'm sorry," I said.

"I shouldn't be telling you any of this."

"I understand," I said, "kids have to be hard for you."

"It's all hard, but this one is for the best," when she looked up at me again her eyes were hard. "But I shouldn't be telling you."

"I'm sorry," I said again. It was all I could think of.

"Comes with the territory," she sighed.

I felt foolish about my hesitancy in the hallway. She had to deal with the agonies of this ward every day, and had no idea about my Carrie.

"Nurse Bonner..." I said.

"Susan," she said, correcting me. The corners of her lips turned upward, ever so slightly, before her mouth became set again in the thin hard line it had been before. "What did you want to ask?"

"Nothing," I said, "It's just I lost my wife in a place like this." I didn't even try to tell her it was the *same* hospital.

"My turn to be sorry," she said.

"Thank you...Susan." She nodded as I took the chair, placed it next to Randy's bed and sat down.

Nurse Bonner turned to go, but hesitated. "You know, I'm really not supposed to talk about the other patients like that. I don't usually, but..."

"It can't be the easiest job."

Her sigh was answer enough. "It sucks sometimes," she whispered. She took another step and turned again.

"I won't say anything," I said, anticipating her words before she spoke.

"It isn't that," she said, holding her clipboard close, "I just wanted to tell you, for what it's worth, I think your brother is going to make it."

Your brother.

I was just about to correct her about it, but decided not to. In many ways, Randy *was* my brother.

"Thank you. I'm glad to hear that," I said. "He's had enough bullshit in his life already, but he's a good guy. He deserves a chance."

"Well, his injuries were extensive and the tests he's been undergoing having been rather rigorous, so Doctor West has had him in an induced coma, but he's slowly bringing him out of it."

"That's good, right?"

"We'll know for certain in a few hours."

"This Doctor West," I said, "he's a good doctor?"

"One of the best."

"Good," I said, "Randy deserves it, if anyone does."

She nodded and went out to finish her rounds, while I sat and looked at Randy, wishing with all my heart there was something I could do besides watch the gauges and the ventilator-induced movement of his chest. I suppose you could say I prayed for him, but it wasn't really praying. I don't know if I could do that for anyone any more.

Watching him lie there, I couldn't help but think again of all the carnage I'd seen in my life. The war, a murderous stalker, and Carrie's final moments. All that, and a madman back in my own hometown. Now this.

I couldn't help thinking about all the mayhem and suffering that's followed me...and my friends...everywhere for so long. I know I'm not supposed to dwell on it, but if you've never seen war up close, or felt the panic that comes from tragically losing friends and loved ones, it's an easy thing to be argumentative and brave about it. If you have, it's hard not to despair.

It isn't just that the memories are often hard ones. It's also that words don't seem capable of doing justice to the horror of it.

Life can be like that, too. It's often a war all by itself. The worst of it brings back a host of unwanted memories.

As I sat alone in that sterile room watching my friend, I lived a lot of them all over again.

CHAPTER 24 - Joe Candleman

The neighborhood around Cherry Street was going through a lot of changes. At the end of the previous year, the County Sheriff had started to beef up daily patrols of the area. This year, the patrols went from once a day to every four hours. Business, which had never been terribly good, was down. Way, way down.

Going Out of Business signs, which had been hanging for a long time in many shop windows, now blossomed in most of them. Many were already closed.

The big bosses didn't like it one bit.

Every storeowner on Cherry Street had counted a lot on the casual shopper. After all, it was the *hippie-wanna-be's*, rich kids with money, usually looking for pot, who helped us make our quotas. Hard-core dopers seldom had any spending cash and were usually more trouble than they were worth.

That had all fallen away, because regular patrols by the fuzz tended to discourage all those snot-nosed rich kids. They were too afraid Daddy might not bail them out if they got busted. Their answer to that fear was to stop coming around at all.

Big Sam and his main henchman, Train, had been gone for a long time, so they didn't have to deal with it. The bosses all took it out on me. Who else? They'd already made it clear they were going to close down the whole Brickdale-area operation, if things didn't improve...fast.

"We miss Big Sam," they told me.

Me, I didn't miss the fat pig...not one bit. Sure, he treated me well enough while he was the big boss, but he was capricious, ya know? When that car bomb took him out at his country club, it was a blessing...sort of. Moved me up the ladder, that's for sure. But being the center of attention and the guy responsible for the bottom line certainly added a lot of pressure to my life.

Losing Train had been another story. He was a guy I could trust, and it was a damn shame he had to go the way he did. Unlike Sam, he had been a big loss.

I really missed him.

Then that *creepazoid*, Micah, came in and took over Sam's spot. I thought the big boys sent him, so I stepped aside, but it seems he just came waltzing in on his own when he got out of the slammer. Made himself at home in Sam's old place...like he owned us, or something.

By the time I realized he had no real claim, it was far too late to do anything about it. The big bosses put up with his intrusion because he was bringing in money again, and, just like in the legit businesses, profit is the bottom line...or should I say the Holy Grail.

People are funny like that. Good or bad, they will put up with anything, if there's a decent buck in it. They'll even tolerate a boatload of bullshit, if the money is good enough.

I thought I'd been doin' okay handling things, and was pissed at being shoved aside like that, but I would never dream of saying anything. What could I say? I thought the big bosses had sent Micah.

From day one, I never cared for the asshole, but people in this crowd who said such negative, critical things out loud too often had a disturbing tendency to disappear.

Like forever.

The whole area around Brickdale had never been wildly profitable. Big Sam had run it with an iron fist and got just enough to soothe the money brokers, but with his right-hand guy, Train...and Big Sam himself...gone, the big boys talked a lot again about getting out. I kept telling 'em I could run it, but with my numbers I was obviously just a little fish to them; one who wouldn't be missed, but didn't want to leave.

Micah showed up and soothed 'em for a while. Then he messed with those Camron brothers again, the same ones that got him sent to the slammer in the first place.

Now he was gone again, too.

While I would always think of Micah's demise as *good riddance*, the bosses in Chicago and New York were not pleased. They were getting more than a little antsy about our whole operation. I knew if they shut it down and I had to move anywhere...anywhere at all...I'd be just another worker ant. One almost certain to get squashed by one of the bigger bugs, if I got out of line.

I confess I was thinking a lot about moving somewhere on my own anyway. Dreaming about it, I guess you could say. It was something I indulged in a lot. The fantasy was often the only thing that kept me going all day.

When the bell over the front door tinkled, it ended my daydream for that day. I looked up to see Philly walk into my shop with Little Tony.

Philly had always been a low-level putz...not known for his sparkling intellect. I was surprised to see him with Tony, who was a pretty good enforcer in his own right.

"Look what the cat dragged in," I said.

Philly giggled his stupid, nervous little laugh, but Tony stared at me like he wanted his eyes to cut me in half just for breathing. I think Tony resented me being in charge of anything at all but, like the rest of us, didn't want to say anything to piss anyone off...just in case.

"Thought you might want to see this," Tony said. He threw an old copy of the local Brickdale daily rag on the table. When I saw it, I was surprised. It talked about those dudes Micah had got himself all shot up about.

Brickdale Authors Book-Signing Tour.

The article itself wasn't much, but it mentioned the two Camron brothers...the ones that Micah unsuccessfully tried to eliminate. It seemed they were doing really well.

"Why should I care about this shit," I said, "This is out on the west coast."

Philly giggled again until I scowled at him.

"Show him the other one," Philly said. He was waving his arm at Tony like a petulant little girl, "Go on...show 'im."

Tony laid down the current edition of the same rag.

Local Brickdale Author Seriously Injured in California Plane Crash.

I looked at it without saying a word, and Philly started his silly giggling again.

"Joe," Little Tony said, with a smirk on his face that his smoldering eyes didn't share, "you always were a little slow on the uptake, weren't you?"

I thought he was treading a little heavy across the line with that comment, but Tony could be unpredictable and dangerous, so I decided to keep my mouth shut.

"Whattya want me to say?"

"Those creeps got Micah put away, and now they're worth some dough," Little Tony said, "and their itinerary for several weeks was laid out, day-by-day. That alone, to me, made it worth reading."

"Yeah," Philly piped in, "and now we all know exactly

where they're gonna be for weeks...the hospital."

"So, whattya want me to do?"

Philly shuffled his fat body nervously, hopping back and forth from one foot to the other, while Tony lit a smoke.

"Shouldn't we maybe contact some of the boys on the west coast?" he said, with a silly giggle. "Better yet, we could hop on a plane ourselves. Go out there and take care of it. I figure those two might be ripe for a little retribution, if you know what I mean."

Little Tony had an evil smirk on his face as he nodded.

"Wasting those two isn't going to bring any money to the till," I said.

"No," Philly agreed, "but icing those guys, whether or not you see any dough from it, would certainly go a long way to solidify your position."

Out of the mouths of babes.

CHAPTER 25 - Janice

We both paced the front porch like skittish cats while we waited for a cab to arrive to take us to the airport. When it finally pulled up to the curb, I marveled at how fast Donnie seemed to calm himself.

Within moments, none of his nervous fluttering or stammering was evident at all. On the contrary, his demeanor would have told anyone he was a person in complete charge of his life. *Just like before.*

"Capitol City Airport," he said, before I could even open my mouth. He gave the cabbie directions to the proper terminal without so much as a blink. Then he handed the man two twenties. "This is extra, above the fare and tip, if you get us there fast."

The cabbie's face visibly brightened, as he shot away from the curb. Even with that admonition, it still seemed to take more time than usual to get to the airport. I wasn't sure if it was just in my mind, or something real caused by the orange construction barrels that seemed to be everywhere, clogging traffic. I wondered why nothing ever seemed to get fixed. I kept checking my watch, certain we were going to miss the flight, but I was probably too upset to be thinking about our travel time objectively.

"Why are they always working on the damn roads?"

"Relax, Jannie," Donnie said, patting the back of my hand, "we're doing fine."

When the cab finally pulled into the airport departure lane, I was surprised when I checked the time. We were early. Donnie paid the cabbie and got us inside the terminal, where we waited in a seemingly interminable line.

"C'mon, Janice," he said, as he trotted in front of me after we got our boarding passes. "They've must have started boarding by now. We've got to hurry." He ran with a long, loping stride and I did my best to keep up with him.

I was out of breath when we reached the gate leading to the plane's gangway. No one else was in the boarding line area at all. I was afraid we'd missed the damn thing until a stewardess came out the door to the portable gangway.

"Are you the Camron's?" she said. I was too winded to do anything but nod. "Good. We've been waiting for you. Some of us didn't think you were going to make it. You only had about three minutes to spare. We were just getting ready to seal the door. I'm glad you made it."

"Me too," I managed to choke out.

The woman leaned close to me. "Just between us," she whispered, "you're actually late, but I took my time closing up just now. I won a twenty-dollar bet. I said you were going to make it."

Donnie took my hand and led me down the gangway. "Never a doubt," he said, grinning.

"Seats twenty-two A and C," the stewardess said, as we passed behind her and entered the plane. One of the other attendants closed the door after we got in.

Some of the people already on board clapped as we took our seats. I was a little embarrassed and wasn't sure they were all glad for us because we made it, or were being sarcastic about our late arrival delaying their takeoff.

There was a woman between us in row twenty-two, but she seemed very happy to let us squeeze in and give her the aisle seat. Donnie let me take the window.

"You two must lead a charmed life," the woman now in 22-C said, as she re-buckled her seat belt.

"Not so anyone would notice," Donnie said, flashing her his great smile and a wink. "We got lucky...this time." I couldn't help admiring his old charm, which was back.

"Well," said the lady, a great smile on her face as she rubbed Donnie's arm, "Let me grab just a tiny bit of that luck. I could use it."

"Take all you want," Donnie said. "It hasn't been very good to me lately."

"Oh," she said, "having problems?"

I leaned forward so she could see me. "You might say that," I said, more snippy than I ever intended, trying to discourage her. The last thing I wanted was a lot of chit-chat on the flight.

"Marital?" she said, looking at me and then at Donnie, being far too nosy. I know she was imagining something sinister going on between the two of us.

"It's my brother," Donnie said, "he's in the hospital."

"My husband..." I added.

"Oh-h-h," She said, making the one word sound like it was several syllables long. "What's wrong? Is he ill?"

"He was in an accident," I said.

"Oh, dear," the woman said. "At work, or in a car?"

"Listen..." I started to say.

"His plane crashed," Donnie said.

When Donnie said that, the woman sitting next to him said, "Oh, dear," again. Then she rubbed his arm one more time, as if she was trying to give back whatever luck she might have received the first time.

The woman sitting in the seat across the aisle whispered to the man sitting next her, and then glared at both of us as she crossed herself.

I could imagine that an invisible wall had been erected around us as people nearby, who had seemed so interested in our arrival, now actively leaned away from us. Other than the other stewardesses, who hadn't heard Donnie's remark about a plane crash, no one bothered to talk to us. Most wouldn't even look at us.

"Gee," Donnie whispered to me, after we were in the air, "that went well."

I knew from his grin the people didn't bother him, and he was trying to ease my mind, but it wasn't working. All I could think about was Randy.

"I'm so scared," I said, watching my hands tremble.

Donnie put his hand over mine and I saw his head nod, but his only sound was a long sigh. I knew, for all his bravado, he was worried, too. The flight from Capitol City to San Diego was less than five hours long, but I was certain it was going to seem like forever.

CHAPTER 26 – Joe Candleman

I decided to go take care of the Camron brothers myself. At least that's what I told that lamebrain, Philly. Truth is, the day after Philly and Little Tony confronted me, the big boss in Chicago called me direct. Something he never did.

He scared the living shit out of me when he told me, in no uncertain terms, to get my fat ass out to San Francisco on the double. He had been so pissed when he found out those two Camron brothers were still running around, freely sucking in air, he could hardly talk in full sentences.

I got the gist of it though.

Randy Camron and his brother were toast.

At least, they had better be...and soon. Micah had promised to take care of it, and failed miserably. That was never going to fly. You gotta understand, the guys we work for hate failure and never, ever take 'no' as an answer.

Not more than once.

Micah had let them down, so now they wanted my ass out west pronto. They even sent a private plane to haul me out there. That's when it sank in to me how important this was going to be. Not waiting for a commercial flight meant my own ass was certain to be fried if I should fail.

I was only mildly surprised to find Little Tony waiting for me in the plane. He did a poor job of hiding the fact he wanted to be Number One in town, instead of me. Most of my time in the last several months had been spent making sure I was two steps ahead of him.

"Why are you always dressed like that?" Tony wanted to know the moment he saw me.

I looked down at the tie-dyed t-shirt, cargo pants and sandals that I almost always had on.

"I like being comfortable..." I said, "...what of it?"

"You look like something that stepped out of a bad 60s movie," Tony said. "Look at you. Those clothes. That bald head of yours...that greasy fringe that passes for hair." He snorted a little before he said "No one wears a fringe like that down over their shoulders anymore."

When I heard him rant like that, some of Micah's words about the quality of our help came back to me.

Gave me one doozy of a headache, ya know?

"What are you doing here anyway?" I ignored his put-down but couldn't keep the contempt out of my voice.

"Got my orders," Tony said, almost cavalierly. "I don't think the boss man trusts you, Joe."

"Tell him to get screwed," I said.

"You really don't want me to do that."

There was not a trace of humor in Tony's face.

"No," I said, surprised at the shakiness that found its way into my voice, "I guess I don't want you tellin' him nuthin'."

"Didn't think so," Tony mumbled.

He laid an attaché case on the seat, dialed in a number for the lock and opened it. For a moment, my heart raced. There were guns inside. Two of them. Tony took what I assumed were silencers and threaded one onto the business end of each weapon. When he was done, he handed one of them to me.

"Careful," he said, "it's loaded."

He took a couple of innocuous white plastic cards out of an envelope lying in the case, put one of them into his wallet while handing me the other one.

"What's this?" I said, looking at the card. It had a logo on one side of, alongside the words *Scripps Memorial Hospital.*

"Access," Tony said, and for the first time ever...I saw him smile. I found it unnerving.

"Access? To what?"

He pointed at the hospital logo. "Whattaya think," he said, adding *asshole* under his breath. "You didn't imagine we was gonna just walk into that hospital and announce ourselves, did you?"

"Where did you get these?" I said.

The look of utter disdain he gave told me it was a stupid question to ask, even before he answered me.

"Let's just say it pays to have connections."

I watched him put his gun in a holster that he already strapped around his shoulders under his sport coat.

"So, that's it? We just waltz in and waste those guys and walk back out?"

"Something like that," Tony said. He took the card from me and held it up in front of my face. "This little ticket gets us into...and out of...secure areas," he blew on it and wiped it on his sleeve, "without any hassle."

"I sure hope you're right."

"I don't get paid to be wrong."

I hefted the gun he had given me. "Better show me how to work this," I said, "I'm used to revolvers."

The look on Tony's face again told me how stupid he thought I was, but he didn't say anything. Instead, he took the gun away, showed me how to eject the clip, reload and reinsert it into the handle.

"I suppose you know what the trigger looks like?"

"Of course."

"Will wonders never cease," Tony said, mocking me.

"Listen..."

"This is the safety," he said, flipping a little lever on the side of the weapon and ignoring my glare. "When it's up like this on a Glock .45 the safety is off, so be careful you don't shoot your damn self."

He spent the next hour going over the use of the gun, again and again.

"Listen," I finally said, "I got it."

"Yeah, sure," Tony practically snarled at me.

"I can handle it," I said.

"I hope so," Tony said. "You realize we might have to waste a few witnesses, too."

"Got no reason to off anybody but those two perps."

"Whattya living in, Candy Land?" Tony said, "Anybody spots you, of course you'll have a reason. That is, unless you want to spend the rest of your life in the slammer, or worse, after someone you *don't* take care of fingers you."

"I don't like wastin' innocent folks."

"You're pathetic, do you know that?"

"I just don't see..."

"Shut the fuck up, Candleman. Look, I'll go in first and take care of the marks. You just guard my back."

"I still don't like it..." I said.

There was fire in his eyes as Tony snapped at me. "Just keep your sorry ass in front of me then, damn it." He pushed me hard to move me toward the door, and that added to my surprise. No one I knew ever touched a superior that way.

"What the..." I started to say.

"I told you to shut up, Candleman. I ain't gonna have you bumbling around and shooting me in the *f-ing* back."

His statement stopped me again in the middle of my sentence. The thought of shooting him hadn't occurred to me as a serious thought until that moment, but it was going to go through my mind again soon enough.

CHAPTER 27 - Janice

Donnie was once again magnificent. He struck up conversations with the people around us, and I watched in awe as their aloof and adversarial attitudes seemed to melt like snow in warm sunshine.

When we landed in San Diego he was so much like his old *always-in-charge* self, without once being the least bit pushy or obnoxious, I was truly amazed. He was charm personified as he got us off the plane, through the concourse and down to the luggage carousel in record time.

As I stood there watching him, I couldn't help thinking about how far he had come. My husband had doted on his little brother when he needed help, and I knew Donnie would do his best to do the same, now that his big brother was the one in trouble. *Trouble?* Once that thought entered my mind, it was all I could think about.

Even though I was on my way to him, I was so worried about what had happened to Randy, I started to tremble. *Is he all right? I don't want to lose him.*

I couldn't help it when I started to cry, right in front of everybody. The lady from the plane, the one who had rubbed Donnie's arm for luck, was right behind me. She put her arm around me. "I'm sure your husband will be all right, dear," she said, "Trust in the Good Lord."

When she said that, my sniffling turned into a wail. Donnie put his arm around me, never seeming to notice all the people who were staring at us. "It'll be all right, Janice," he said, "Randy's a tough old bird."

I wanted to believe him. I needed to.

"Here," he said, pushing me gently forward, "help me watch for the suitcases. Ours are black."

Most of the suitcases were black, and I knew he was only trying to keep me from focusing so much on Randy, but I didn't object. I needed something to do to keep my mind off what might be waiting for us at the hospital.

God love him, it actually worked. Donnie's calm voice encouraged me, and I was so caught up in watching the conveyor I didn't see Roger Craig until he has almost right there beside us.

"Hello Don...hello Janice," he said as he got close.

I jumped. So did the lady from the plane, who almost dropped her suitcase. Roger's voice was quiet, but he was right beside us when he spoke.

"Omigod, Roger," I said, my heart racing. "I didn't know you were here. You scared me half to death."

Roger looked like a little boy who had just been scolded. "I'm sorry, Janice. I didn't mean to frighten you."

I took a deep breath. As I looked at him my mind was suddenly full of a million questions.

"It's all right," I said, "I'm okay. Really. Have you heard anything? How's Randy doing?"

"Haven't heard anything yet," Roger said. As he shook hands with Donnie, he looked back at me and shrugged. "I got a call from Paul to pick you two up. He said he was going to the hospital to be with Randy." Roger was wringing his hands together. "I haven't heard anything else. I was hoping you knew something more."

Donnie turned away long enough to grab our suitcases from the carousel. "Whattya say," he said, turning back when he had the handle of one in each hand, "we head over to the hospital and see for ourselves?"

"Sure," Roger said. "By the way, I took the liberty of reserving rooms for both of you at a nearby hotel. I figured you were going to be out here for a while." Roger nodded his head toward the suitcases. "We can stash the bags there on the way over."

"If it's all the same to you," I said, trying hard to keep my tears in check, "I'd rather to go see Randy first." I needed to see him. The hotel and my luggage were the last things on my mind. "We can put the bags away later."

"Of course," Roger said. "I understand."

He motioned for us to follow him, but we had only gone a few steps away from the luggage carousel when we heard someone shouting. We would have been able to ignore it except for one really disconcerting little thing...they were shouting *our* names.

"Janice...Donnie! Is that you?"

Looking down the long row of luggage returns, I could see, waving frantically next to a sign announcing a flight just coming in from Tuscaloosa, two very unexpected people. Our old friends, Puz and his wife, Tammy.

Tammy was running and waving, calling our names. Puz was moving toward us, too, at a fast trot, but his bad knee made his movements appear awkward.

"Omigod, Janice, it *is* you!" Tammy blurted out even before she reached us. She threw her arms around me and gave me a hug that almost knocked me over. "I'm so sorry about Randy. Have you heard anything? How's he doing?"

Puz repeated the greeting when he finally caught up.

I didn't answer any of their questions because part of me couldn't believe our old friends were actually standing there in front of me.

"What are you two doing here?"

They both started talking and it was hard to follow either one of them. "We heard about the plane crash," Puz finally said, "and thought you might need some support,"

I could have hugged him.

155

"So, you came all the way out here from Alabama," I said, "but why? I mean, I love ya to pieces for it, but haven't you already been through enough with us?"

At that moment, Puz gave me a long look I will always remember. "We all grew up together," he said. "You guys are like my family...and you shouldn't be alone for this."

Tammy stood beside him, nodding.

"Okay, family," Donnie said, taking charge again. "Let's get our hellos and hugging out of the way, get to the hospital and see about Randy. We can talk about our reunion later." His brief comment didn't lighten the moment for anyone, a realization I could see in his face.

"I second that," Roger said. Under his breath, he added, "Good thing I rented a van." He looked at the group, and I watched the grimace he gave us turn into a timid smile.

No one returned it at all.

The ride to the hospital was one of the most surreal trips I've ever made, and that's saying a lot. No one talked. Not a sound. After Roger said "Here it is," when we got to his rented van, none of us said another word. We rode in absolute silence.

I thought of the agonizing ride to the church for my mother's funeral, holding my weeping father's hand. I also remembered the trip my late step-brother made taking me to the hospital when I was having my baby. I can still hear Anna telling him *Go now!* The only sound during that miserable ride was my own howling with every contraction, and Albert's strained voice telling me I would be okay. My mind also flashed back to the long, silent ride to McDermitt's Funeral Home for Albert's wake, after they shipped his body back from Vietnam.

I remembered, too, a few moments of utter joy, riding in the limo beside Randy from the church to our reception. Every bad thing that had ever happened to me seemed to be gone, while I was sitting next to him that evening. At least, before Micah showed up, it was a beautiful memory.

That was the thought that actually bothered me the most. It was scary to think those few moments might have been one of the last good memories I would have.

CHAPTER 28

The silence during that drive was overpowering. No radio played. No words were spoken. Quiet staring dominated everything. The first words anyone spoke for half an hour were once again from Roger, telling us we'd arrived at our destination. "Genesee exit," he said, his soft words sounding loud after the awful silence. As we got off Interstate Five, he added, "Scripps Memorial Hospital is ahead on the right."

The road curved around to the right from the exit, until we saw the angled, multi-story wing of the Prebys Cardiovascular Institute, which was the first building off Genesee, leading to the imposing complex of the hospital.

My heart felt like it was in my throat, and I found it hard to breathe. I felt lost, like I had so many times already in my life. "Oh, God, I don't want to be here."

"Jan, this is where Randy is," Donnie said. He reached over and held my hand, while he said it.

"Oh, I know, I know," I said. "I just wish none of this had happened. I really don't want to be here."

"None of us *wants* to be here, Jan," Puz said, "but we need to be here for Randy." I looked up at him and he added, "We're also here for you."

I looked around at all their solemn faces and realized how blessed I truly was. "Thanks guys," I said. There really wasn't anything else I *could* say.

We parked in the massive lot and walked, single file, toward the complex. I couldn't help thinking we must have looked like a troop of condemned prisoners as we marched toward the huge concrete overhang that marked the entrance to the building.

Once inside, our footsteps seemed muffled by the decorative carpet that led to the waiting area and the tidy alcove at the back that held the *Information* desk.

"We'd like to see Randy Camron, please." I managed to get those words out before I got so choked up I couldn't speak any more.

"This is Randy's wife, Janice," Donnie said, stepping up beside me and touching my shoulder, "and I'm his brother."

The receptionist looked down at her ledger. "Mister Camron," she said, "seems to be quite the popular fellow."

All things considered, I thought it was an odd thing to say. "What do you mean?"

Everyone else was silent again, seeming to wait on her next words.

"Well," the receptionist said, looking down at her notes again, there's a Mister Barrett with him now, there were two reporters here earlier, trying to get up to see him...and now, all of you."

"You didn't let them go upstairs, did you?" I said, "The reporters, I mean."

"Of course not," the receptionist said. "Mister Barrett was quite adamant about keeping them away, too."

Thank you, Paulie, I whispered to myself.

Donnie was biting his lower lip, and had already turned toward the elevators. "May we go see my brother now?"

"You're all family?" The receptionist pointed to Puz, Tammy and Roger.

"Yes, we are," I said, before anyone could contradict me.

She sighed. "That elevator over there. Room 733," she said. "The ICU nurse will direct you once you're upstairs." As we all piled into the elevator, she added, "Good luck." She seemed to sincerely mean it.

I knew the building was air-conditioned, but it seemed awfully hot and my heart was beating at a furious pace, as we went upstairs, to see Randy.

CHAPTER 29 – Joe Candleman

When we arrived in San Diego, Little Tony had an unpleasant surprise waiting for me. Parked to one side of the hanger doors was a windowless white panel van. I was looking for the black limo that was our usual ride, so I didn't pay it much attention.

"Over here, asshole," Tony barked, standing next to the driver's door of panel van, "Hop in."

That was the first moment I paid enough attention to read the words written on the side of the van's white panels: *Medical Waste Disposal, Inc.*

"What are we doing in that thing?" I asked.

"Getting up close and personal," Tony said. "Here, put this on." He handed me a white hospital jacket while he slipped one on himself. Each jacket had the *MWD, Inc.* logo embroidered on the front left side.

"I don't understand..." I said.

"You didn't think they were going to let us just waltz into the place, did you?"

"I wasn't sure what your plan was," I admitted.

"You don't plan much of anything, do ya, Joe?"

I was ready to give him everything that was running through my mind at that instant, but one look at his eyes...cold, staring, emotionless eyes...and I knew I would be best served by keeping quiet.

Tony drove to the hospital, took a drive marked *service entrance*, and parked the van in the alleyway between two imposing buildings. Grabbing a heavy-looking duffel bag from the back of the van, he used the magnetic pass cards he'd obtained to open the security lock on a metal door marked *Hospital Personnel Only*, and gain entrance.

"Now what?" I said, peering into the doorway over Tony's shoulder. There was a large, flat table with drawers and cupboards on the far wall, right beside another locked door. To my immediate right was the beginning of a flight of stairs, dimly lit by a single bare bulb on each landing.

"Now we climb." Tony stuck his head inside and looked around before gesturing to me and adding, "the ICU is on the seventh floor." I heard his footsteps on the metal stair treads in front of me as he started upward.

We had gone four flights up when Tony paused.

"You ain't very popular with the boys upstairs anymore, Joe," Tony said. "I suppose you know that."

"Times been rough."

Tony laughed, or at least he let out a long, sustained *hrmmf*...sort of like a chuckle, something he rarely did, not being the happiest person on the planet you would ever want to meet...and started up the stairs again.

"No lie," Tony said, with another little chortle, "times been rough? I wonder why?"

"I done my best."

"Think that's enough?" Tony said.

"You seem to have a pipeline to what the boys upstairs are thinking," I said, "Why don't you just go right ahead and ask 'em about it."

"I already done that," Tony halted his climb.

"What did they tell you?" I was a little afraid of what his answer might be.

"Well, for one thing, they're going to shut down the whole Cherry Street operation." He seemed almost smug. "I tried to get them to turn it over to me, but Micah and you have soured them on the area ever being a good producer anymore." He sighed as he said, "So, they're going to move further west. New town. New customers. New rules."

"How's that going to help anything?" I said. It was an effort to keep the distress out of my voice.

What was I going to do if they closed up shop?

"First off," Tony said, "it'll be *my* town, with no old farts getting in the way, hanging onto things that used to be." He paused to light a cigarette. "Know what I mean?"

163

"Not exactly."

"C'mon. old man. I know you ain't stupid. The Camron Brothers are my primary targets out here," Tony said, gesturing up into the dark stairwell, "but my secondary assignment...which gives me no end of joy...has always been to get rid of you, Joe."

I saw Tony's right hand slip into his jacket. To say I had anticipated him would be giving me more credit than I deserve, but I was pretty proud of myself for being ready. As he turned, I could see his weapon was drawn, but I couldn't keep the smile off my face.

I let off a short burst from my own silenced Glock 37. It was already pointed up at Tony and the nearly noiseless, semi-automatic discharge now ripped into his abdomen and chest at close range.

"Guess it's still my town, wise guy," I said, watching him fall. "Oh, and thanks for the refresher course. Don't know what I'd have done without it."

There was a look of stunned surprise in his eyes, which never closed. When he was crumpled and still, I pushed his inert form down the stairs with my foot. Tony's body slid at first, then it tumbled down the stairs, leaving a liquid red trail spattered down the steps...and an echo that seemed to take a long time to go silent.

CHAPTER 30 – Sticks

Maxie kept rolling her eyes at me as I tried to convince the stubborn hospital receptionist we were related to Randy Camron. "Look," I said, "my name is Strate...William Strate. Randy is my...cousin." I could have kicked myself for the momentary hesitation that said I was unsure of the relationship.

"I'm sorry, Mister Strate," the receptionist said, "I'm afraid I can't let you go upstairs. Your name isn't on the list of relatives or friends approved to visit."

"Terrific," I said, "but how about Maxie here...she's his, um, sister. Surely she's allowed to see him."

The receptionist looked at her list again. "I'm sorry, Mister Strate, neither one of you are on the list...and until a family member who *is* arrives to vouch for you, I'm afraid I can't let either one of you go upstairs."

"Well, damn it," I said, trying to make it clear how upset I was, "who *is* on the blasted list? If we knew who already had bloody access to Randy we could at least be watching for someone we knew."

The woman gave me a look that said she would just as soon shoot me as answer, but she glanced through her list again. "I have Mister Camron's wife, Janice. His brother, Don. A Roger Craig. Mr. and Mrs. Ken Pozanski...and a Paul Barrett," she said, before closing the book on her desk.

She folded her hands and watched me, as if I was going to make a break for the elevator, or something.

"That's it?"

"That's all I have," she said. "They're all here, and they're already upstairs."

"Puz and Paulie are both on the list?" I said. "They're already upstairs? How is that possible? They're not relatives. Hell, they're not even neighbors anymore."

"Mister Camron's brother and wife brought them," the receptionist said. Her lips were a tight line across her face.

"Can't you get in touch with them?" I said. "Let them know I'm here. We came all the way from New York."

Maxie started to say something, but I cut her off with a wave of my hand. The receptionist glared at me, and seemed almost relieved when her phone rang. She answered it and turned her back on me.

"Look, hotshot," Maxie said, rapidly losing interest in my less-than-perfect ability to fast-talk the receptionist into letting us upstairs, "You work this out. I'm going to the lady's room to powder my nose."

Her impatient comment irked me no end, but I had to smile as I watched the heads of all the men in the lobby turn to follow her crisp, stiletto-tapping march as she strode toward the ladies' room.

No matter how hard I tried, I didn't make any progress toward getting upstairs. I could see other people in the lobby watching me as I pleaded with the woman. A few of them were smiling and pointing. No matter what I said, the receptionist wouldn't even turn around to look at me. She was still on the phone when Maxie returned.

"Look," I said, when I heard Maxie's heels clicking on the floor again, "Do I have to speak to your supervisor to get some attention around here?"

The receptionist put her phone down and slowly turned around. She could have been a poster-child for the phrase *daggers-coming-out-of-her-eyes*, but she didn't say anything. She didn't get a chance. Maxie spoke to her first.

"Honey," she said to the receptionist, with both eyes on me, "I know he's a skinny, obnoxious prick, but underneath it all he's got a heart of gold...and we really did come all the way from New York. I know Randy and his family will want to see us, every bit as much as we'd like to see them. Please, be a dear and get us up there, if you can."

The receptionist's face softened. She cleared her throat and turned away from me toward Maxie.

"I was just about to tell the...gentleman...here, that Mister Camron's brother has been told you've arrived...and he said I should send you right up. Room 733."

Maxie hooked her arm in mine and pulled me toward the elevator. "C'mon, *Sticks*," she said, sounding more like my Mother than my girlfriend, "you've annoyed the lady long enough."

CHAPTER 31 - Paul

I had been sitting alone in that damn, sterile little room for several hours. That's harsh to say, since Randy was there, too. Sort of. He never spoke. He never moved. Doctors and nurses came by at regular intervals to check his monitors, but what they were recording, I could only guess.

None of them seemed to be in any mood to discuss anything, and I wasn't about to bother them with small talk. Only a few of them even nodded to acknowledge my presence, so I spent most of my time watching Randy's face and hands for some sign, however small it might be, that he was conscious or awake again.

Nurse Bonner eventually returned with another doctor whom she took the time to introduce.

"Paul, this is Doctor Raymond West. He's the physician overseeing Mister Camron's care."

Doctor West was tall and good-looking, with a shock of tight, dark curly hair. My first impression was he seemed far too young to be in charge of life-and-death decisions for someone, but he was composed, polite and professional, and he seemed very optimistic about Randy's condition.

"I'm glad you're here," he said, shaking my hand with a firm grip. "I'm sure you've been told we put your brother in an induced coma to treat the worst of his injuries."

He went around beside Randy's bed without seeming to wait for an answer. I looked at Nurse Bonner, who had to be the source of his "brother" statement. She just smiled a little and shrugged.

"Now that he seems beyond the worst," Dr. West said, putting the stethoscope to his ears and listening to Randy's chest, "we're bringing him out it."

He paused, as if I was supposed to say something.

"Will he be okay?" I was surprised at how weak my voice sounded.

"I believe so," Dr. West said. "He should be able to talk to us very soon. He can tell us himself how he feels." He put his fingers on Randy's neck, checking the carotid artery. As he did, he looked up at me. "It will be good for him to see a familiar face."

"So, he's really out of the woods?"

"There's always the possibility something could still develop that needs our attention," Dr. West said. He paused to clear his throat. "We'll fill in his wife completely when she arrives, but I don't suppose it will be a problem to say I'm confident he's going to be fine."

When the two of them left, I sat alone again watching Randy, hoping the doctor was right.

After what seemed like an eternity, Nurse Bonner stuck her head in again. She had another smile on her face as she pointed at Randy and said, "It seems Mister Camron has some additional visitors."

I expected to see Donne and Janice when they walked in, since I had been waiting for them, but I was surprised at the others who followed Roger Craig into the room.

"Omigod," I said, "*Puz!*"

Puz and his bride were the last people I expected to see, and the handshakes and hugs took a while to finish.

"Good to see you, Paul," Puz said. He pointed toward the bed. "How's he doing?"

Janice practically ran to the bedside. "Did they tell you anything? Is he going to be all right?"

"Dr. West was here a little while ago," I said, talking more to Janice than anyone else. "He said he'd fill you in when you got here, Jan, but he seemed to think everything was going to be fine. Randy should be awake soon."

"I have a hard time seeing him like this," Donnie said. He sat in one of the chairs and put his forehead to his hand. Janice stood beside the bed, stroking one of Randy's arms.

Puz and Tammy stood at the foot of the bed, and I could tell they were both having a hard time watching Randy. I have to admit, the way he was hooked up to all that machinery was frightening, at best. It reminded me so much of the time I spent in this same building with Carrie on the night she died, I wanted to go out into the hall where I could be by myself and weep.

Roger Craig stood by the door, taking it all in, his lips pressed into a hard line. After several minutes, he came across the room and stood next to me. He put his hand on my shoulder. "How are *you* doing, Paul?"

I put my hand on his and did my best to smile at him. "*Dodger*," I said, "Sometimes being a friend is hard work."

He nodded, and I remembered him being the first one there for me that night with Carrie.

"I'll second that," Puz said.

Donnie looked at each one of us in turn and said, "I'm willing to bet the vote right now would be unanimous." Donnie's sigh hadn't ended before we heard Janice gasp.

"He's moving!" she said, her voice a high-pitched squeal. She put both hands on her husband's chest and said it again, louder. "He's moving!"

At just that moment, Randy moaned, the first sound I'd heard him make in all the hours I'd been there. It was, at once, both encouraging and frightening.

"Nurse! Nurse!"

I could hear Roger Craig out in the hallway, shouting. Nurse Bonner came rushing back in and slapped the button on a red-colored speaker on the wall above the bed.

"Dr. Allcome, Room 733," she said, "Dr. Allcome, Room 733." She looked at me, her face tight, and added, "It's a code for all available support."

Several doctors and nurses arrived within minutes and the room got very crowded. Politely, but firmly, they asked all visitors to move to a waiting room down the hall. Janice, crying, excused herself, disappearing into the ladies' room.

CHAPTER 32

When almost an hour had passed, I walked back down the long hallway to see if all the turmoil surrounding Randy a little ago had abated.

I couldn't hear anything, which I hoped was a good sign. Peeking in, I could see the doctors and nurses were gone. Randy was indeed awake, sitting in the bed, propped up with pillows. All the tubes had been removed from his throat, and all but one of the intravenous connections seemed to be gone.

Besides the monitor measuring his heartbeat, the only evidence of his accident that remained were the small bandages and pinpricks on his arm, the shaved side of his head...and, of course, the bruises around his left eye.

"Glad to see you up and about," I said. I was lying, because, in truth, I thought he still looked awful.

My voice must have startled him. He jumped, and for a moment I could see panic in his eyes.

Closing his eyes and taking a deep breath, Randy's voice sounded raspy and dry. "Hi, Paulie," he said, trying to force a smile, "I guess that makes two of us." He kept looking toward the door, as if expecting someone. I was pretty sure I knew who it was he was looking for.

"You seem jumpy. Do you need the nurse?"

"No, you just startled me. I didn't know anyone was with me. You the only one here?"

"Of course not," I said. "Janice and Donnie are here, too. Couldn't make 'em stay home."

Randy didn't acknowledge my attempt at humor, but he seemed to visibly relax when I told him his wife and brother were there.

"How long have I been out?" he said, his voice soft.

"It's been a couple of days."

"Is Janice okay? Where is she?"

"She's worried about you, lunkhead. What do you think? She flew out here with your brother as soon as they heard about the crash. I was already close, so I came to hold down the fort until they arrived. She's down the hall. They chased us out when you started to wake up."

Randy motioned for me to sit down. "Thanks, Paulie," he said, "I owe you one."

"You don't owe me a thing, buddy. I'd have done it even if you didn't have half a head of red hair."

He ran his hand over the recently shaved side of his pate. His smile revealed a newly chipped front tooth.

"You've always been there for me," he said.

"I don't know about that," I answered, embarrassed.

"You have," Randy said, "at least until your old man moved you out of Brickdale."

"A lot of the guys were there for each other," I said. "I didn't do anything special or unique."

"Sure, you did, Paulie. Lots of times."

"Right," I said, even more embarrassed. "Like what?"

"Do you remember that time they were building a new house on the sandlot where we used to play baseball?"

"Mister Giles sandlot," I said. "How could I forget? After he built a house there we had to play ball in the street."

"You always had chalk for the bases," Randy said.

"That was from my old man, not me."

"It was you as far as we were all concerned."

Funny what a twelve-year-old thinks is important.

"You were still always there for me," Randy said again. When I didn't respond, he added, "Have you forgotten the mountain on the sandlot?"

The mountain.

That was what we called the huge mound of dirt the excavating machines piled up when they dug the basement for Mister Giles' new house.

"You saved my life there," Randy said.

As soon as he said those words, I remembered what he

was talking about. All the kids in the neighborhood had been playing in the yard, whooping and laughing as we scrambled around the pile of sand. As it got close to sunset, parents started calling the kids home. Randy's mother had called him and his brother, and Donnie had left already. I knew my mother was going to call me in for supper soon, too.

Randy and I were the last kids still playing, and we scrambled up *The Mountain* together one last time. I reached the top first, beating my chest and proclaiming myself King.

"Paulie," Randy said just below me, sounding both winded and afraid, "Help me, I think the sand is shifting."

I had reached down and grabbed his hand, just as the whole side of the pile of sand shifted, sliding back into the hole dug for the basement.

"Holy shit," Randy had shouted. "I coulda been buried under all that sand."

I remembered what I said to him.

Good thing I was here, I guess.

"Like I said," Randy repeated, "You saved my life."

"We've been through a lot," I whispered.

"I'm glad you're here now, too," Randy said.

"You have quite an entourage, you know," I said, wanting to change the subject. "Roger Craig is here. So are Puz and Tammy. They're all just down the hall with Janice."

"Puz and Tammy are here?"

Nodding at him, I was just about to head to the waiting

room to tell everyone Randy was awake and ask them to join us, when Nurse Bonner came in.

"There's a young man downstairs," she said, "who one minute claims to be Mister Camron's cousin and his brother the next...and he says the young lady with him is Mister Camron's sister. He's pretty adamant about it and is starting to make a scene. Should I call security to take care of them, or let them come up?"

In my life there are few people who could have that kind of effect so quickly. Randy and I looked at each other and we both said the name at the same time. *"Sticks!"*

Randy grinned at me. "Now cut that out," he said, wagging a finger at me. "You know it's my brother and I who are nicknamed *The Twins.*"

"Of course," I said. "Who was it who named you?"

To Nurse Bonner, who looked bewildered, I said, "By the way, let 'em come up...they're family."

Randy nodded. "Yes," he said, "they certainly are."

The nurse shook her head slightly, rolled her eyes and went back out the door.

I was right behind her.

"You're not leaving already, are you?" Randy said.

"I've got to get Donnie, your bride and the rest of them, and tell them you're awake," I said. "If Sticks is here, we're going to need all the backup we can get, just to counter his ego." Randy was laughing out loud as I trotted down the hall. It was a good sound to hear.

178

Janice had not yet returned when I got back to the others. "Randy's awake," I told the group.

"Thank God," Donnie said.

"Where's Janice?"

"She hasn't come back yet."

"Do you want me to go get her?" Maxie asked.

"Thanks for the offer," I said, "but no...she doesn't even know you."

"I could wait for her," Roger said.

"You guys go to Randy," Puz said. "I'll wait for her."

"You sure?" I asked.

"Yeah, let him," Donnie said. "Janice knows him, and she's going to have a zillion questions. Plus, she knows he won't BS her about anything." He looked at Roger and winked. "Besides, Randy just woke up. He could probably do without gazing again on Ken's ugly puss for a few moments."

"I agree," Tammy said with an impish smile. We all laughed when she said it...including Puz.

Even without Janice, Randy's room was getting very crowded again by the time Sticks arrived with his girlfriend.

"Hello...anybody home?"

I heard Sticks voice before we saw them. *Same old Sticks*, I thought. I would have recognized his distinctive voice anywhere. However, when they walked in, I had to do a double-take at the girl with him. Dressed in a skin-tight navy dress that ended mid-thigh, and wearing tall, stiletto heels, she looked enough like Janice to be her sister.

Randy, by his greeting, must have been confused by her appearance, too.

"Hi, hon...what did you do to your hair?" he said, with a confused frown. He tried to reach up from the bed and take her hand, but she was too far away.

Puz walked in before Maxie had a chance to answer, and I watched a scowl form on his face. "Where the hell did you change clothes?" he said to Maxie, as he looked back out into the hallway.

"Wait a second...that's not Janice," Randy said.

"Of course it is," said Puz, his scowl deepening, "but how did she get here so fast?"

"Puz, Paulie...Donnie, Randy," Sticks said, with a nod toward Roger Craig, "I'd like you to meet *my* friend, Maxie." Everyone could tell, by his mile-wide grin, he was obviously enjoying every moment of what was going on.

When Janice did walk in a moment later, still dabbing a tissue around her eyes, Sticks strutted over to her.

"Hi, Jannie," he said, "It's been a long time."

He put his arm around her waist, and his hand rode low down on her back. I saw Janice's lips tighten, along with her shoulders.

"What do you think you're doing?" she said.

"Just saying hi to the prettiest girl in the room."

"Move your hand, or lose it," Janice said, stepping away from him.

"Hey, cut that out!" Randy yelled at him.

"You want I should smash the asshole for you, Randy?" Puz made a slow grinding motion with his right fist against his left palm, just like he used to do when we were all kids.

"Look," Sticks said, cringing as he realized he was in trouble, "it was an honest mistake."

"Honest?" Puz said. "Like you would know honest if it bit you in the ass."

"Well," Sticks continued, "how *was* I to know Janice would be upset by a little *touchy-feely*? After all, Maxie loves it when I do that to her."

Most of the room was glaring at him, and Maxie's eyes were full of hurt as she slapped him.

"Man," I said, unable to suppress my grin, "I'm glad things with this group are back to normal."

CHAPTER 33 – Joe Candleman

When I reached the seventh floor, I had to pause to catch my breath. *Not as nimble as you used to be, are you, Joe?* I used Little Tony's swipe-card to open the door to the stairwell and, as silently as I could, stepped out into the hallway on the ICU floor.

There was not a soul in sight.

This is too easy.

I thought I might be able to find the room, waste the two Camron brothers and sneak back out the way I'd come in, without running into anyone at all.

That thought went away entirely when I rounded the first hall corner. I was still orienting myself to the sequence of the room numbers when a young guy, either an orderly or a janitor, pushing a wringer wash bucket in front of himself, came out of one of the rooms.

"Hey," I said, "Which way to Room 733?"

He turned and pointed down the hall to his left.

"Thanks," I muttered.

"It's around the corner," he said, "but, hey, deliveries are supposed to get checked in on the first floor, then go to the nurse's station here on seven. You aren't even supposed to be up here, are you?"

He was reaching for the walkie-talkie clipped to his belt when Tony's words came back to me.

We might have to waste a few witnesses, too.

I realized no matter who he was summoning, it would mean more people to deal with, and it would certainly cost me the benefit of surprise.

"What's your name, kid?"

"Bill," he said, pointing to his name tag.

"Sorry, Bill," I said. "It's just business."

I put two rounds into him, watched his eyes grow wide with surprise when they struck, and then watched him fall.

Checking the hallway in both directions, I put a third round into his chest, then dragged his body back into the room from which he'd come. I used his mop to wipe up the red smear on the floor and, when I was done, shut the door to the room.

So far, so good.

Once that was done, I got back to the whole reason I went all the way out to California...getting rid of the two Camron brothers stoolies, clearing my reputation and maybe...just maybe...saving my job. Philly's words came back to me and, sighing as I remembered them, I had to wonder why everyone at home thought so little of him.

Icing those guys, whether or not you see any dough from it, would certainly go a long way to solidify your position. That was the phrase that sent me on this quest in the first place.

As I tiptoed down the hallway, I could hear a murmur of voices ahead of me. I made sure the safety was off on my weapon, and once I turned the corner I saw it.

Room 733.

From the many voices I heard coming from inside, it seemed Randy Camron was doing well and already receiving visitors. *Too bad.* I hoped his brother would still be in there with him, to save me a trip.

CHAPTER 34 - Randy

J anice had a few choice words for Sticks, who had the decency to look mortified at her chastisement. However, Sticks making an ass of himself, upsetting Janice, and embarrassing Maxie and the rest of us all seemed to be moot issues when Joe Candleman walked in.

I'm sure the rest of them didn't know who he was, but I recognized him from my trips to Cherry Street for Donnie, when my brother had needed help.

Trying to buy weed from him, the man had seemed an ominous a figure to me, back then in Brickdale. He was far overshadowed by the vicious thug with him, Micah, who had also appeared at our wedding like some sort of avenging demon. I wondered what the hell he was doing so far from his normal haunt.

Joe's dark, oily hair was still shoulder-length and stringy, and I watched light reflect in different patterns off his shiny bald spot as he turned his head. I didn't think his being here was any omen of good, and had to stifle a gasp as I saw him move the gun tucked in his waistband swiftly into his fist, as if to confirm my fears.

"You two," Candleman said, waving the gun at Paulie and Donnie, as he pointed at the group around the other side of my bed, "move your asses over there with the rest."

They both moved immediately, but Paulie stumbled when his foot hit something under my hospital bed. I heard a metallic clatter. From the momentary look of panic that crossed Candleman's face when he heard it, I thought he was going to shoot both of them that very instant.

"Just stand still, asshole," Candleman said. He licked his chapped lips as his gaze shifted from Paul to the others in the group, and back again.

"Ain't this a nice little party?" he said.

"What's this all about, Joe?" I said.

"There now," Candleman said, "You remembered my name. I thought sure you'd have forgotten all about me by now. It's been a while..."

"You helped me help my brother," I said, "I haven't forgotten that."

"So, you repay me by putting me out of work?"

I threw my hands up over my head. "I don't have the slightest idea what you're talking about."

"That's what they all say," Joe muttered, "but Big Sam and Micah are both gone, aren't they?" He paced back and forth, muttering about someone named Tony, his gun sometimes pointed right at his own chin.

"Look," Donnie said, "Why not help *my* brother now?" He pointed at me and shrugged.

"Nice try, kid," Joe said, "but him and you...both of you...have to go. I got no job to go home to, if you two live beyond today."

"Omigod," Maxie said.

"You believe in God?" Joe asked her.

When she nodded, he pointed the gun at Janice and Tammy and asked the same question.

"Of course," Janice said. Tammy nodded.

"Then I suggest you start praying," Joe muttered. "cause I got to waste the lot of you."

"No!" Puz shouted.

"Oh, I don't want to," Joe said, still looking at Janice, "specially cute girls like you...but I got no choice."

He looked at everyone in the room, in turn. "Ya see," he continued, "I already wasted Tony, but that can work to my advantage, so I don't really mind. Ain't gonna miss that slob at all." He sat for a moment in the chair nearest the door. "The janitor," he said, standing up again, "that was a shame, but he had to go...no witnesses, you see?"

I saw Paulie grab the rail at the head of my bed. "I've gone through bullshit like that before," Paulie said. "More than I care to remember. You really don't have to do any of it...but you're going to, aren't you?

"It's a real shame, you know," Joe said, looking first at Paul, then Maxie, Janice and Tammy, "having to waste you and these nice ladies here...when all I really need to do to square myself is get rid of the Camron brothers."

I sensed, rather that saw, Paul edge to the corner of the bed, with little between him and Sticks. "Played any baseball lately, Sticks?" he said. It seemed to me for all the world like he was trying to draw Joe's attention.

It was that exact moment that Mango, the pilot from my ill-fated flight, walked into my hospital room.

"Hey Randy, ole boy," he practically shouted, "they told me you were awake now, and I came up to see you before I get discharged from this place. How you doing?"

There was no report...only a muffled *pffft*. His face took a moment to register surprise when Joe shot him and a red blossom appeared near his left shoulder.

"Ground ball to short!" Paulie suddenly shouted. I watched him kick my empty metal bedpan across the floor, as Joe turned and fired again.

CHAPTER 35 - Paul

As I listened to yet another madman who'd come into my life explain how he had to kill all of us, I knew I had to do something to stop him. As he spoke, this *Candleman* character, who Randy seemed to know, waved his gun around. He was pointing it at the women in our group when a red-haired guy came into the room, calling for Randy.

"Mango," Randy shouted when he saw him, "No!"

I watched a red blossom form on Mango's shoulder as Joe fired at him, and knew my time for planning was over. I had to do something...now...or it was going to be forever too late...for all of us.

"Ground ball to short!" I shouted, trying to divert Candleman's attention. As I shouted, I kicked the empty metal bedpan beside Randy's bed across the floor. It was skittering like a hot grounder toward him when Sticks, reacting exactly as I had hoped he would, scooped it off the floor with one hand and pegged a perfect strike across the room. It struck Joe Candleman hard, square in the middle of his forehead.

"Nice one, Sticks!" I shouted.

Joe's dark, stringy hair seemed to flair out behind him as his head snapped backward from the force of the pan hitting him, but he managed to get off another shot before he dropped the gun and crashed to the floor, and I felt the sting of the bullet as it tore into my shoulder.

Puz dove over the fallen Candleman and grabbed the weapon. He scrambled to tie the man's hands behind his back with a bedsheet, but I realized he didn't have to hurry, because Joe Candleman was out cold.

Randy dialed security from the phone at his bedside, shouting into the receiver as soon as someone answered, "There's a man with a gun in room 733!"

I was impressed with hospital security, as sirens went off almost immediately. I wouldn't learn until later that it was just about that time a regular service delivery team found Tony's body on the stairs, and alarms started ringing all over the hospital.

CHAPTER 36

When we all got released from the hospital, I had Janice, Randy, Puz, Tammy and Donnie spend several weeks with me at my house in Cielo. Sticks and Maxie even stayed for a few days. Mango stopped by once, too, and we had a great visit. He has one hell of a sense of humor. Upset by the two passengers who died in the crash, he decided to give up flying. "At least with anyone else in the plane," he said.

Roger stopped by often, too, and we had many pleasant days together. It was, in many ways, like old times. I grilled a lot on the big porch overlooking the valley, and the bunch of us would talk and laugh late into the evening. It was one of the nicest times I've had since Carrie died.

Then, when Randy got the all-clear to travel, Janice, Randy and Donnie all headed back to Brickdale.

Once my friends left, and I had to spend a night alone again, something became very clear to me.

I cannot stand being alone in this house.

Just that fast, my mind was made up. I started making phone calls before noon the next day. I set things in motion and kept on writing, but never said a word.

About a year later, with Joe Candleman still in jail, Roger sold another book for me. The advance was the largest one I'd ever received. The day he came over for me to sign the papers, I told him what I was planning.

"You're going to sell the Cielo house?" he said. "You're crazy, you know that, don't you?"

"I can't stay here anymore, *Dodger*."

"Where are you going to move this time, Paul?" His exasperated sigh told me all I needed to know about his thoughts. I knew before I said anything else the news I had for him was not going to sit well with him at all.

There was a big change coming.

"Well, I've had a real estate agent working on it, and he's already bought several properties for me."

"Okay, I'll bite," Roger said, "where?"

"Brickdale."

"Brickdale?"

"On Reichold Street, actually," I said. "Effectively, I bought the whole damned block."

"The whole block?" There was disbelief in his tone.

"Yep," I said, "the block next to it, too."

"You're kidding."

"You know me better than that, Roger," I said. "Do I sound like I'm kidding?"

"What are you planning to do?"

"That's just it...I've already done it. I had an architect draw up plans for a gated community, containing several large houses."

"You what?"

"I've also had my lawyer petition Brickdale to have them sanction the proposed changes to the neighborhood."

"You're kidding?"

"You said that already," I smiled, as I chided him. He didn't smile back.

"Have you heard from them yet?"

"Yes," I said, "They approved it."

"When did you do all this?"

"In all honesty," I said, knowing he would be upset at me for keeping such a secret, "It's been in the works for over a year now. It's almost done."

"You're serious. You're really moving, aren't you?"

"Yes, Roger," I said, "I am."

"Brickdale?" he said with a tone of disbelief.

"Yep."

"Gonna miss you, Paul," Roger's comment came out as a long sigh. I had expected something else from him.

"There are going to be a few extra houses," I said. "One of them can be yours, *Dodger*, if you want it."

"It's a nice offer, Paul," Roger said, "but my business, my clients, my friends, are all out here."

"I'll be in Brickdale," I said, trying to catch his eye. "Are you going to stop being my agent because of that?"

"Well...no..."

"Then think of it as a vacation place," I said. "Randy and Donnie are coming, too. That gives you three clients right there in town, whether you think we're friends, or not."

Roger chuckled a little to himself.

"I've even talked *Puz* into moving back home," I said, as an afterthought.

Roger's laugh was now almost a bark.

"How'd you ever manage that? I thought he was dyed-in-the-wool Alabama by now."

"I promised him a new house for his mother," I said, "at the far end of the neighborhood."

"This I've got to see," Roger said.

"Come with me," I said, "I'm going out there to talk to the architect."

"When?"

"Tomorrow," I said, "My plane this time."

I could tell before *the Dodger* answered I was going to have company.

194

CHAPTER 37

Roger rented a car as soon as we arrived, and we drove straight to the architect's office. Looking at the plans, it was obvious the roads were going to be quite different on the northeast side of town.

The railroad switching yard at the far east end of Reichold Street was long gone, but several of the small manufacturing buildings remained along the north-south street that used to bisect that end of the neighborhood. Some of the buildings were still occupied, but most of them were vacant.

I didn't care.

I had a landscaper put in a large stone wall, about twelve feet high, all across the back of the new gated community, effectively sealing off any entry from that direction. When I was satisfied with it, I then had him plant a veritable forest, about forty feet deep, in front of it all to hide it.

"There aren't that many homes in there, Paul," Roger said, looking at the plans. "I remember lots of them when I was here before."

"All of them little, working-class houses," I answered, "but look at these." I pointed to the structures penciled into the new neighborhood and handed him the plans for one.

It was for a spacious, open-concept ranch-style home, with a large yard. The specification box in the bottom right corner of the plan said the house proper was more than 3500 square feet.

"I've got a house there for Puz and Tammy just like that one," I said, "He got a job as the football coach at the high school, and they've already started picking out their furniture."

Before Roger could say anything, I smiled at him and added, "At the other end of the block is the house for Mrs. Pozanski. It's a little smaller, but she's actually moved in already. She's officially our first tenant."

"Where's Don Camron going to be?" Roger asked.

"Right over there," I pointed on the plat in the general direction of Mrs. Anchor's old property. I didn't bother to tell Roger about any other history of the area, or the flowers she used to grow. He wouldn't have known who anyone was anyway.

"Where will Janice and Randy be?"

"Right in the middle of the block," I said, "Just about where Janice used to be before. They'll have a place like that one," I said, pointing at the plan in Roger's hand. "Anna and Kevin are going to move in next door to them."

"There are several more houses on the plan," Roger said. "Who goes in those?"

"One is for me, of course...near where my old house stood. Just cross the street from Randy and Janice."

"I would have thought this big unit near the front gate was yours," Roger said. He had a smirk on his face that told me he was ready for my comeback.

I'm sure I disappointed him.

"That big building near the entry gate is a community center for the whole neighborhood," I said. "There'll be a kitchen, a big dining hall, a place for a live band, a game room with pool tables, card tables and toys for the kids."

"Kids?" Roger said, deadpan.

"Someday," I smiled.

"And these others?"

"One is for Sticks, if he wants it," I said, "although I doubt he'll coming back any time soon." When Roger cocked his head at my comment, I added, "I asked him, but he likes it in New York. He's *somebody* there. Let's face it, Bill never did enjoy being the skinny kid everyone around here knows as *Sticks*."

I looked around the new neighborhood, imagining what it would be like someday.

"One is yours, too," I said, "if you want it. The other few places are for new people, to keep us from getting to be sticks-in-the-mud."

"Seem like you thought of everything," Roger smiled. "How much are you asking?"

"Nothing."

"What?"

"Just like with all my friends," I said, "if I offer it to you, it's free."

"Say that again."

"You heard me. It will be titled in your name, with the mortgage completely paid." Joking with him, I added, "Of course, you'll have to pay your own property taxes."

"Why would you do this?"

"Would you believe," I said, "it's because I enjoy your company so much."

"There's got to be more to it than that."

"Roger," I said with a sigh, "some of the best days of my life were spent here in Brickdale. Except for Carrie, some of the best friends I'll ever have came from right here in this town. What's not to like about it?"

"I have to admit, it looks nice on paper."

"C'mon," I said, "get in your car. I'll show it to you."

As Roger drove, I was looking at the familiar streets and buildings, giving him directions. Roger was silent, for the most part. He glanced at me every once in a while, as we approached our destination.

"Another dead-end street?" he said as we arrived. "I thought that was one of the reasons you wanted out of the Cielo house?"

It was something I'd said to him often, but for a vastly different reason. Literally everything in California was a dead end for me, without Carrie. Part of me was afraid there was no place on Earth where that wouldn't be true.

Still, I looked around after he said it and realized he was right, in a way. Reichold Street, which used to intersect most of the larger streets in the area, now started and ended at its new western gate...the only entrance into or out of the new subdivision.

"Kind of looks that way, doesn't it?"

"Reichold Boulevard?" Roger said, reading aloud from the bold new sign on the gate that said, *Reichold Boulevard – Private*. His right eyebrow arched upward like it usually did when he asked a question.

"City demanded it," I said, "I wanted to keep the same name, but they claimed the neighborhood no longer fits their definition of *Street*...so we compromised."

I punched in the code to open the gate so we could drive down the wide, new, tree-lined boulevard that separated the brand-new houses on either side. I couldn't suppress my grin as I watched Roger take in the small baseball field that had been constructed in the grassy center median. It looked like it had just been mowed, and the silver bleachers on each base line glimmered in the sun.

"Nice touch," Roger said.

The landscaping for most of the houses was done, and everything had a fresh, new look. The ancient golden maple that had once been in front of Mrs. Murphy's house really stood out. It was huge now.

It was still there because I had always liked that old tree, and I would see it from my new front porch. It was originally scheduled to go, but I had the architect re-draw the plans to move the ballfield, so it wouldn't have to be cut down for first base on the new diamond. I wished the oak tree that once stood in front of my old house was still there, even if we didn't need its gnarly old roots to hide big pieces of chalk in anymore.

"I think this is the nicest neighborhood I've ever seen," Roger said as we drove in. "It's like a bloody perfect picture."

"I put in all the good things about it, and left out all the bad," I chuckled. "God knows we've all seen our share of the bad already. Of course, I did ask *you* to come."

"You know what?" Roger said, after a moment, "Maybe having another place out here would be a nice idea." He winked at me. "Price is right, after all."

We drove slowly through the whole place. When we reached the roundabout at the east end, we paused for a moment and looked at the new woods before we headed back toward the gate.

"All right," he said, "which one is mine."

I winked back at him and turned to look at what was

essentially a new, upscale neighborhood in my old home town. "You saw the plans," I said. "Pick one."

"I kind of like that one by the ball diamond."

"Good choice," I said. "It's got plenty of room for a home office, it has two guest rooms and it's close to all your Brickdale clients. If you're sure, I'll have papers sent to your lawyer tomorrow."

"Thank you," Roger said.

As he waited for the gate to rise so we could leave, I couldn't resist kidding him. "There's something about free that does sound nice, doesn't it?"

"Don't congratulate yourself too much," Roger said, "there's always been a cost to knowing you." He punched my arm, and his smile made me know he was kidding, so it took the sting out of his next words. "How long do I have to keep it before I'm allowed to sell?"

"You can turn it the same afternoon, if you like."

"Not a chance," he said, poking my arm again. His grin was enormous. "Thank you, Paul."

I looked back at the neighborhood again, liked what I saw and, for the first time in a long time, actually felt good again. Really good.

Maybe I'm not turning around on a dead-end street, I thought. I had been worried about that since my new plans started. *Maybe I'm finally going home.*

* * *

ABOUT THE AUTHOR

Ron Herron is a member of *Michigan Writers*, the *National Writers Association*, the *Association of Independent Authors* (US), the *Alliance of Independent Authors* (UK) and the *Academy of American Poets*. He once worked for some of the world's largest advertising agencies and an international Fortune 10 company.

The winner of multiple writing awards, he lives and writes in Michigan with his lovely wife, an ugly mortgage and one extremely large cat.

AUTHOR'S WEB SITE:
www.ronaldherron.com

FOLLOW THE AUTHOR'S BLOG:
www.rlherron.com

LIKE THE AUTHOR ON FACEBOOK:
https://www.facebook.com/rlherron

LEAVE A REVIEW ON AMAZON
http://amzn.to/2qQDCzz

Made in the USA
Middletown, DE
13 August 2017